A Dance In the Desert
The Story of Leah, Jacob, and Rachel

By L. M. Roth

Table of Contents

Chapter 1
Leah's Tragedy

The day was broiling. Summer was at its peak with no hint of relief in sight until the autumn rains came, a full two months away. A lone cloud overhead gave false hope to those hoping it might multiply and produce others that would birth a refreshing shower to drench the parched landscape. But the cloud hung stationary in the sky over the endless vista of plains from which occasional rocky hills rose up to break the monotony of flat land. The grass had taken on the dull and listless look of July after two weeks of no rain coupled with intense heat, even drying up in places, the ground baking to hard earth from which dust rose at the slightest breeze.

A fly buzzed near Leah's ear. Wearily she waved a palm branch to swat it away. Beads of sweat dripped down her forehead onto her brow. A drop fell into her eye, causing it to sting and burn.

She hated flies. It was a fly that had caused her disfiguration. She remembered all too well the day when she had been transformed from a pretty young girl to one whom men averted their eyes from as she walked past.

It had been a day similar to this one. She had sat with her mother Adinah on the porch watching her sew garments that would be worn by the children of the servants. Their mothers were far too busy with their duties and so it fell to the lady of the house to provide for their children.

Leah remembered thinking that it was a good thing that her mother genuinely loved children and therefore made attractive garments in cheerful colors that were a joy to wear. She knew of other women who grudgingly doled out the dreariest garments in the drabbest hues of tan, gray, and ecru for the servants and their broods. Not so the garment in her mother's hand; a miniature robe dyed in a brick red shade with a matching turban. How delighted the little wearer would be!

Just then, however, an angry buzzing distracted their attention from their occupation. Glancing up, Leah saw a swarm of flies that had descended on the lunch that was waiting for her and her mother on the table. It was their custom to eat out of doors when it was hot so that they might catch a refreshing breeze. But today's repast looked as though it would be devoured by flies before they could even take a nibble.

"Oh, no, you don't!" she exclaimed, and leaped up from her chair to swat away the swarm.

She cried out as several of the flies buzzed directly into her face. She attempted to chase them off but before her mother could come to her aid she had felt the sting of their anger as she received bites on her eyelids.

It was her mother who rescued her. She took the injured and weeping girl into the house and applied compresses of warm water. But it was to prove to be ineffective to be of any real aid...

The local doctor had examined Leah's eyes

as soon as he was fetched for by a servant who hastened to obey his mistress's frantic instructions. He tut tutted and wore a frown as he opened the swollen lids as gently as he could. Leah's soft cries awoke pity in his heart, and he did his best not to hurt her.

But there was no remedy for the pain his diagnosis would give the pretty young girl.

"Well, Miss Leah," he stammered as he cleared his throat. "It might have been worse. You could have been blinded. Those flies had evidently visited other places before they attacked your lunch."

He paused, and Adinah hung on his words, the anxiety in her eyes wringing his heart. No woman wanted to hear what he was about to impart.

"The truth is," he started over, "that the infection will eventually clear up and you will be able to see without any impairment. But those flies carried disease with them, and the swelling of your eyelids may be permanent."

Leah gasped and her mouth dropped open as she stared at him. Horror clutched her heart, and made it stop beating in her chest.

No! she silently cried. How can this be so?

It was evident that her mother was as stunned as she was. Why *her* daughter? the anguished look on her face cried out all too plainly as she clutched Leah to her chest and dropped kisses on her thick black hair as she gently stroked it.

The doctor could only shake his head in pity. He tried to alleviate their distress as best as he could.

"It may *not* be permanent," he soothed in a voice far softer than they were accustomed to hear from him, "but it may, with time and care, be reduced and your lids return to normal. Only time can tell."

He knew of few cases where such a miracle had happened, yet it was possible. He only hoped that in Leah's case it might be true.

As for Leah, the diagnosis was a tragedy. She was thirteen years old, and more than one village lad had cast an admiring glance in her direction. She was slim and well-formed, with a womanly figure already revealing its shape. Her oval face with its delicate features was enhanced by the linen mantle she wore over her long black hair as shiny as the wings of a raven.

True, her younger sister Rachel was already at eleven considered to be the beauty of the family and would soon outshine her older sister as the sun does the moon. But Leah had an attractive daintiness and feminine charm that forecast it would be no difficulty to obtain a husband for her.

Alas! That forecast had now been changed.

Bitterness smote her heart as Leah remembered back to that day three years ago and how it had changed her life forever...

Her eyelids were no longer as swollen as they had been when she first was attacked, but her eyes were left with a tendency to water easily. Although her other features were unimpaired and were quite pretty, framed by the tresses of her thick shiny hair, she bore the stigma of one who was considered diseased, and as a result no offers came to her father for her hand in marriage.

Overnight she had gone from an attractive maiden whose future seemed secure, to a young woman whose future was doubtful and full of uncertainty. Where she had once taken marriage and motherhood for granted as an assured part of her life, Leah now faced the fact that she may never participate in these rituals of womanhood, for which a woman's life seemed to have no other purpose. For if she did not marry, of what value was her life in the eyes of those around her?

She knew that only healthy and attractive women were easily married off. Men viewed such as good for childbearing, and pleasant to look at when not actually engaged in efforts to obtain more children. Indeed, their lovely appearance was considered a credit to their husbands, whose manhood was confirmed by his ability to win such a woman for his wife.

Leah sighed as she realized that she was doomed to a life of loneliness. What man would possibly want one who was disfigured? All too quickly she answered her own question. Only the lowest class would take such a one, and her father would never permit her to marry beneath her station; for that would reflect poorly on him, as if he could not do better for his eldest daughter.

And if there was one thing that mattered in life to her father, Laban, it was the way his image was reflected in the eyes of the world.

He was a man of no great esteem in their city of Haran, where they lived on the outskirts, where they had plenty of land to feed his flocks. It was in Haran, however, that their life in the community was established, and where they mingled with the citizens. They were welcomed by their neighbors and greeted with friendliness, but not treated with the exalted respect of those in high positions.

But Laban yearned to accumulate much wealth and rise to a higher status among the people of the city. His flocks of sheep and goats were adequate to feed his family and his servants, and they lived in great comfort, but he coveted gold and fine possessions. Haran was a lush city on the plains of the Tigris River. Here the soil was rich and the grass grew green and plentiful, where his flocks could graze to their hearts content.

Haran itself was rapidly growing, attracting the attention of those who were weary of a nomadic life and who wished to expand their social life by mingling with a more extensive population. Here in its limits they could make desirable matches for their sons and daughters, and perhaps provide them with a more comfortable lifestyle and greater prosperity than it had been their own fate to realize. In the city they could trade their goods with others, and in so doing they were exposed to the greater world around them as they met those from lands far away that many of them had never heard of as they wandered through the deserts and wilderness where the only company was the wildlife or occasional other nomads with whom they might share a meal or travel a short distance until their roads parted.

Merchants flocked to Haran, visualizing enhanced opportunities for trade. They brought with them finely woven textiles and perfume from Egypt, sought after by the wealthy to proclaim their affluence, and pottery skillfully crafted and greatly in demand by wives who used it for everyday mundane purposes such as carrying water from streams for household use, and beads and shells strung on string that were of no value except to adorn the necks and wrists of eligible maidens, enhancing their beauty as they drew attention to slender throats and delicate hands.

That Haran would one day become a center of commerce and culture was already evident in the burgeoning growth of its citizenry and their desire for wealth and refinement. It was also a city where the populace honored gods of their choice, rather than bowing to one patron deity as did the cities of other regions. Leah's own father, Laban, had his own collection of household idols, called teraphim, which he consulted daily for guidance and in which he put much stock regarding their counsel. There were times when the teraphim had been proved right, such as when Laban's father, who made his home with them, had been struck with a sudden illness that took his life before night had fallen.

The idols had fallen face down when Laban took them from their hiding place (he did not trust them with anyone else; so certain was he that others would wish to consult them and thereby steal them from him), which signified death, he informed his startled family. And it was not long after this announcement that his father complained of vertigo and weariness, with burning pain in his head. He was found to be burning with fever and put to bed. His attendants spent many hours bathing his forehead with cool cloths, and fanned him with palm leaves in a vain attempt to make him comfortable. But by nightfall he had breathed his last and been taken from his family.

Leah reflected on these facts as she viewed the landscape before her. Her father, although practical in so many ways, trusted in his idols more than anything in the world. If they spoke, then it must be so. Her sister Rachel also listened to them, although not with the same devotion as Laban.

Leah was more like her gentle mother, who did not seek idols for counsel, but strived to make all those around her happy. Adinah's smile brightened even the gloomiest day, and her sweet voice made music in every ear. Leah was very like her in nature; she hated conflict and raised voices, and was instrumental in making peace when her father and sister quarreled or the servants were seen to mutter when disgruntled by a command barked out by her domineering sire.

Laban and Rachel both had quick tempers that could blaze into fury faster than the flight of the goats as they scrambled up the rocks in the wilderness. Rachel had inherited her father's pride and sense of entitlement, for everything seemed to come easily to her, and there were indeed times when she seemed born under a special star.

The first thing that one noticed about her

was her striking beauty, that caught the gaze of everyone who saw her and made them stop what they were doing just to stare at her loveliness. She glided with the grace of a gazelle and her almond shaped eyes sparkled when she looked out onto the world. She was quick to laugh and enjoyed a good joke or a witty comment.

By contrast, Leah's glance was demure, often dropping her eyes when she was addressed and rarely looking anyone in the eyes, conscious always of her disfiguration as well as possessed of a natural modesty. Her eyes were soft under their disfigured lids, and she was prone to blushes should anyone stare at her. But Rachel was bold and direct, looking a man in the eye as easily as she did a woman, and her brilliant gaze left a man dazed and confused.

Rachel was also strong and healthy with a vitality that kept her active from the time she arose until the time she retired to her bed, a fact that was not lost on men who contemplated courting her. Such as she would bear a man many children and be tireless in the raising of them. It was a task that she looked forward to and she eagerly contemplated the day when she would raise a family of her own.

But for now Rachel spent her days shepherding her father's flocks, leading them to pasture, nudging them back in line with her cudgel when necessary, and generally attending to their welfare. Her father considered it good training for raising a family of her own, and his daughter was rewarded with a healthy complexion and a toned physique, while the constant walking kept her figure trim and supple. Already there were men contemplating her beauty and considering making offers to her father for her hand.

But Leah knew that for her, in spite of being her father's first born and endowed with an adequate dowry, no such offers would be pending.

Chapter 2
The Stranger

A cloud of dust was coming up the rough road that had been hewn out of the rocky hills of the landscape in which Laban's house nestled. The day had been still and sultry without a breeze to stir the trees or bring relief to sweating brows; therefore only the approach of someone coming up the road would stir up a cloud of dust.

But her family expected no guests, so it must be a stranger approaching, perhaps one of the nomads that periodically passed through Haran and its outskirts, seeking the hospitality of a friendly home in which to ask for a meal to refresh them or for shelter for a night that they might be fortified for further travel the following day. She sighed and wished it was not the latter; her father truly hated being forced to share anything with anyone he did not know, preferring to keep it all for himself and his family, and it would only put extra work on her mother who nevertheless bore with such intrusions patiently and warmly welcomed any guest that might pass under her roof.

Leah strained her eyes to see into the cloud, only to chide herself in reproach for the effort. Was it not enough that her eyes watered easily as it was? Why subject them to more discomfort through squinting her eyelids, as if that would help her to see any better?

As the cloud drew nearer she found herself wondering with greater curiosity than usual at the advent of any visitor who was approaching. Her father had announced to his wife and daughters just this morning that the teraphim had forecast a momentous day in the lives of their family, one that would be important and full of portent for what was to come.

Leah was not certain whether she believed this pronouncement or not; there had been times when the teraphim had been wrong. True, they had foretold of the demise of her grandfather when they forecast death, but what about the time when her father had declared that they had foretold famine, causing him to lay aside much grain and store it in his barns, only to have the crops more lush and bountiful that year than they had been in the past decade?

Laban saved face by announcing that saving the grain and laying it aside had enabled him to sell his surplus to traveling merchants and nomads, who appreciated the bounty that they could carry with them on their journeys for the baking of bread over heated rocks while on the road. Adinah made no comment on her husband's philosophical ramblings as he attempted to defend his idols, but she and her eldest daughter furtively exchanged glances with raised eyebrows and dropped their eyes hastily before Laban spied them questioning his reasoning.

So Leah did not take much stock in the prophecies of the teraphim.

Her younger sister, on the other hand, listened to every word her father uttered regarding their predictions; for had they not accurately foretold a death in the family, and their grandfather was stricken and taken from them that very day? She shuddered even now when she remembered it, and shed a tear in memory of his sudden death. From that day on Rachel listened to widened eyes and breath held in awe at every utterance her father pronounced as having come from the idols.

And so for Rachel the teraphim seemed the very oracle of the gods, and their word not to be disputed or held in doubt.

The cloud drew nearer and at last Leah could see that within it was her sister Rachel. But she was not alone.

She led another figure who walked slightly behind her, to whom she kept turning in conversation as they walked along. To Leah's astonishment it proved to be a man. But how could her sister, although she was capable of rash behavior, to be sure, behave so improperly as to bring a young man to her father's house? Young men were always introduced to unmarried maidens through their parents, who arranged social events such as a gathering of neighbors or an invitation to a meal, in order that they could arrange the meeting and oversee it directly.

And Leah gasped and wondered silently as she waited for them to come nearer.

No sooner had they stepped onto the porch than Leah saw the illumination of her sister's face and the sparkle of her eyes, and immediately sensed that the young man had an effect on Rachel. And when she looked away from her sister to behold the stranger she understood why.

A tall and handsome man stood before her. He had thick brown hair that lay in waves upon his brow and curled in tendrils on the nape of his neck. His large eyes were dark and wide set, and framed by well-shaped brows that cut a line of authority across his low forehead. His mouth was generous and his nose chiseled with the straight slope of patrician refinement.

At the moment he seemed extremely weary, his head drooping, but his air was dignified and his bearing erect in spite of his obvious exhaustion. Leah sensed that here before her was one who had seen better circumstances and had never wanted for anything.

"This is my sister, Leah," Rachel announced with barely contained excitement in her voice, "and this is Jacob, the son of our father's sister Rebekah."

Jacob raised his weary head to politely look at her as good manners dictated when Rachel introduced them. Leah's stomach muscles tightened as she waited for the look of distaste that would inevitably be reflected in the man's eyes. To her astonishment there was only a momentary flicker of his eyes before courtesy steadied his gaze, and he nodded his head in greeting as he bestowed a friendly smile upon her.

As for Leah, her breath caught in her throat, and the customary words of welcome were strangled as she found herself suddenly unable to speak.

It was not long before it was evident that in this case the teraphim were proved right. For Jacob's effect on the members of the household of his uncle was immediate and powerful, and the day of his advent would prove to be portentous indeed.

Rachel seemed dazzled by him, and their eyes met constantly over the table where they all shared their meal that evening. Adinah watched this exchange silently as her eyes took their measure of the young man. A slow smile about her lips and an almost imperceptible nod of her head signified her approval of Jacob. Laban had welcomed his nephew heartily and asked for news of his sister and her husband.

"It is long since I had any word from my sister or her husband, but I miss her and I remember Isaac well," Laban said, as his hearty chuckle was evoked over some memory that he did not share with his family. "A man of means as I recall, and not lacking in the world's goods. No doubt he has taken good care of my sister, very good care, indeed!"

And he laughed again as if at a joke known only to himself as he devoured the bread he had just dipped into the gravy set before him. He glanced around the table at those seated around it with a secret delight in his eyes, chewing ravenously at his bread as he did so.

Adinah quickly averted her gaze from her husband and hastily looked down into her lap. Leah failed to see the joke and openly stared at her father, and she and Rachel exchanged puzzled glances. Rachel shrugged her slim shoulders and then turned her gaze back on their cousin, her eyes softening as she did so. Jacob's brow was slightly puckered, but he did not ask Laban for enlightenment as it would have been considered bad manners to ask such a thing of one who had granted a guest hospitality.

"Ah, yes, I remember!" Laban repeated as his laughter slowly died down to a chuckle.

A clearing of his wife's throat caused him to hastily remember his manners and he turned a more sober countenance on Jacob.

"And what of your family?" he asked, as he cleared his own throat after a swift glance at Adinah. "Are they well and in good health? Do they prosper? What of my sister? Is she content in your land?"

The staccato questions rattled from his beefy throat with the rapidity and intensity of hail falling out of a thunder cloud in a summer sky.

But Leah knew that her father was an impatient man and he was bored with the ordinary interaction of polite conversation that custom dictated he must adhere to when extending hospitality to a stranger. He therefore left it to his wife to convey an aura of courtesy and refinement. He was accustomed to those about him tolerating his whims and satisfying them without delay, and chafed at being forced to obey the dictates that were demanded of a good host.

Jacob seemed to sense this, and hastened to answer the older man.

"My mother is very well, and happy among

our people," he replied.

But Leah noticed a small pucker crease his brow, and his lips tightened suddenly. He seemed to sense her stare, and looked at her briefly before addressing his uncle further.

"My father fares well, and is greatly respected. And yes; they prosper and lack for nothing."

"Ah, that is good, good!" Laban exulted.

His swarthy face was wreathed in smiles as he observed his nephew with the greedy appetite of a hungry jackal lurking in the desert for prey.

Leah was suddenly struck for the first time at how closely her father resembled that particular animal, with his thick black hair that seemed to bristle upright on his head, his braying laugh that erupted without warning, and the way his tongue licked his lips in anticipation of his next meal. She found the comparison somewhat disturbing, however, and tore her gaze away from him.

Laban's questioning took an unexpected turn as he continued his interrogation of Jacob.

"And what of your brother?" he inquired. "You have a brother, do you not? A twin, if I remember correctly."

Jacob seemed to flinch at the sudden change of direction in the line of questioning and his mouth tightened into a straight line before he answered his uncle.

He cleared his throat and his voice faltered as he began to speak.

"Yes," he stammered, and cleared his throat again. "Yes, I do have a twin brother,

Esau."

A light flickered in the depths of Laban's glittering dark eyes. His face was suddenly illuminated and his mouth popped open.

"I have it!" he exclaimed. "When my sister was bearing the two of you she was in great discomfort and wondered if there was something wrong with the babe she carried. She inquired of your father's God for the reason why, and she said that she was told that she was carrying twins; and that there were two nations in her womb, fighting one another for supremacy.

"That is what evaded me," he sighed in contentment.

Then he directed his line of questioning back to Jacob once more.

"How did that turn out?" he asked the red-faced young man, who was clearly uncomfortable by his uncle's inquisition.

"How did what turn out?" Jacob murmured.

Laban sighed and slapped a hand against his forehead.

"The two nations struggling in the womb," he replied, in a voice that betrayed his rising impatience. "Do you and your brother fight as you did in the womb, or are you best friends, as is expected and usual of twins?"

Jacob sank further down into his seat before turning his face back to his uncle.

Leah found herself wishing that her father would leave him alone. She exchanged a glance with her mother, who apparently had the same thought in mind. It was apparent to everyone but Laban that Jacob did not wish to be interrogated so thoroughly regarding his family.

Leah knew, however, that her father would not see the matter in this light, or care if he did understand; for although his nephew, Jacob was their guest and a guest must answer any questions put to him by his host. Such honesty ensured the safety of the host and his family for sharing their home with a stranger, and was to be expected in exchange for a good meal and a roof over one's head should they need more than just a meal to refresh themselves. That Jacob had perhaps never heard of that custom was evidenced by his response.

"May I just say that you have a lovely home, Uncle, and that your family is delightful," Jacob said as he hastily sipped from the glass of water at his elbow and saluted his uncle with it as he did so.

Chapter 3
The Sisters

Before the week was out it was clear that the arrival of Jacob was going to prove to be of great benefit to Rachel. The feelings that she and the young man harbored for one another was evident in the way their eyes met and held with a look of delighted wonder, the way their hands brushed one another's as they passed food across the table and met and lingered softly, and the caressing tone in their voices when they addressed each other. It was not long before Jacob spoke to her father.

Rachel related the news to her sister in a daze of exclamations one evening as they prepared for bed.

"Just think, sister," she began in a voice that quivered with excitement, "Jacob has already asked father for my hand in marriage. He agreed to work for him for seven years, with me for his bride as his wages! Is that not *wonderful?*"

Leah's eyes suddenly filled with tears. She tried to stifle the jealousy that unexpectedly flooded her soul as the pangs of hurt inflicted her heart. She knew she should be happy for Rachel, but her congratulations were soured by the fact that no one had ever spoken for *her* hand, or made any offer to her father in exchange for it. A hard lump formed in her throat and she struggled to find words that would hide the sudden wounding of her soul, and congratulate her sister on her good fortune.

"Yes, how delightful."

Leah forced a smile as she viewed her sister through veiled lashes that hid the shimmer of her tears.

"It *is* wonderful!" Rachel exulted, as she tossed back the mane of her black curls that cascaded down her back.

She shook out her hair and ran a comb through it in preparation for bed. She rambled on to Leah as she pranced about the room, oblivious to her sister's pain in the joy of her own good fortune.

"Father asked how it was that a young man of Jacob's family stature should arrive on our doorstep without a pack, money, or possessions. He explained that he was sent from home with a quantity of goods and even money for a bridal dowry, but he was set upon by thieves in the desert who robbed him of everything but the clothes on his back. That satisfied Father because it meant that his family sent him off with their blessing. He would not be so pleased if Jacob had been cast out of the family, as he at first feared when he showed up destitute.

"And Jacob made the offer to serve Father because it will provide him with independent means and enable him to stay here in preparation for our marriage, and not force him to journey back home to replace the goods his family endowed him with. I must say that I am happy and *so* relieved that he will not have to leave me, for any length of time, as that would make my heart sore indeed, if I were to be deprived of his devotion for even a day, let alone the weeks that such a journey would involve.

"Ah, truly, sister; I long for the day when Jacob and I will wed. He said that the time will fly, so great is his love for me, but I can not wait!"

And Rachel twirled around the bedchamber they shared, sending her nightgown flying out around her in a swirl of linen. She giggled and stopped, as her lovely face was suddenly assailed with blushes. She flicked her mane of hair in front of her face to veil it from Leah as maidenly modesty claimed her again, and she giggled into her long black tresses.

But Leah was not embarrassed by the unmaidenly thoughts that evidently invaded her sister's innocent mind. She was too miserable to dwell on such proprieties, and thought only of how wonderful it must be to be loved by the man of your choice.

While Leah had inherited their mother's gentle nature and sweet voice, it was Rachel upon whom she had bestowed her beauty.

As she entered her teens Rachel grew into a tall and statuesque young woman who resembled a marble goddess rather than a maiden molded of humble clay. She swayed with the grace of a willow tree when she walked, which was an easy gliding gait. Her wavy black hair was covered by a mantle or caught up in a turban, which framed her perfect features and drew attention to their exquisite composition. Her nose was neither too long nor too short, and her full lips were expressive; now puckering in discontent or smiling broadly in amusement. Her dark eyes were wide and brightened with a light of vitality.

For Rachel was vibrant and as energetic as her father. She had his zest for life and found it exciting, amusing, and full of surprises. She faced each day with expectancy, eager to see what delight or joy would overtake her, and embraced it fully as the sun rose and beamed into her bedchamber every morning, and savored the memory of it fondly as the moonlight bathed it in a silvery glow after sundown.

For from the day she was born it was apparent that life would be easy for this child, as her loveliness smoothed her way, giving her favor effortlessly with all about her. Women clucked their tongues when they saw her and forecast a bevy of young men pursuing her; men admired her even as a child, seeing in her a potential bride for their sons. Young lads gravitated to her like flies to honey, and even young girls sought out her company because to be seen with her was to invite attention from the young lads.

It seemed that fortune smiled on Rachel even as the beams of the noonday sun graced the flowers of the field, kissing them in a ray of benevolence. All she would need to succeed in life was to hold out her hand and take whatever she desired, was the general consensus. Indeed, this opinion prevailed so extensively that Rachel came to believe it herself, and took grace and good fortune as her due. Adversity and misfortune was a stranger that she did not know, and whose acquaintance she had no desire or expectation to make.

Leah found life a little more difficult and challenging than her younger sister. And all too often the misfortunes that afflicted her seemed to confirm her apprehensions and fears, until all that she saw ahead of her was a future of gloom and uncertainty, with no joy or love to lighten the darkness of the days that faced her.

Until the incident that caused her disfiguration she had been well-liked in their community, popular with the other maidens and respected by the young men. Women smiled their gracious approval upon her and pronounced that she would be a good mother, for look how tender and patient she was with the neighbors' children! It was true that the children liked her and even sought her out, knowing her to be not only kind but entertaining, as she sang to them in her sweet voice like a songbird's, and told many tales from the lore of their people to enchant them when they grew fretful.

The male friends of her father assessed her with favor as a prospective bride for their sons when she reached maturity. Leah always thought before she spoke and was prudent, as a good wife should be, was modest and demure, as a good wife should be, and she sought the opinion of men and respected them, as a good wife should. All in all, she should do well when the time came to marry, was the general assumption.

But when she was disfigured following the attack of the diseased flies, she became an object of pity, as those around her avoided looking at her. They were careful to invite her to every community event, all the while speaking cheerfully to hide their discomfort at her appearance. And then there were those who viewed her as an object of distaste as they chose not to look at her at all and excluded her from their company entirely.

Leah didn't know which attitude hurt her the most. To be scorned and avoided was painful, and she shed many bitter tears over the careless words uttered by thoughtless people, and the deliberate neglect meted out by the hard of heart that inflicted pain upon her soul. But to be pitied was almost as bad, as it revealed that those who felt sorry for her viewed her as damaged goods with no redeeming value, even if she was not responsible for her affliction and could not help the way she looked, as was muttered in condescending tones by those who clucked their tongues and shook their heads as she passed through the city on errands for her mother or in shopping excursions with her sister.

Her mother had been soothing, spending many hours cradling her sobbing daughter in her arms, as she told Leah that she was not to worry; someone would love her for her gentleness and kind heart.

There were men who looked beyond appearance, she informed her, although they were few and far between, it must be admitted. True beauty was inward, she said, and always made itself felt, just as the opposite was true and a heart of wickedness could not be hidden behind a false appearance, though one might try to gloss over it with brilliant smiles that were as artificial as the cosmetics which the Egyptians applied to their faces.

Her father had also laughed off her fears with the hearty bluster in which he habitually faced his world.

She was *his* daughter, he pronounced, and men would be eager to unite with the house of Laban, he told her, as he tossed his head proudly. Why, the offers would be pouring in, because many men wanted to marry their sons to his daughters, and he had but two of them! Just think of all the men that she and Rachel could choose from!

And he slapped Leah heartily on her shoulder, his dark eyes glittering uneasily as he chuckled in a manner that did not convince her of the truth of his words.

But in all the seven long years that Rachel waited as Jacob worked for her hand there was not a single offer that came for Leah's.

Chapter 4
The Waiting

Leah listened to the chatter of her father and the others and moved quietly away from the table where they had just dined. Jacob and the family lingered, engaging in idle conversation and exchanging the news of the day.

She felt weary suddenly, drained by the effort to behave in a cheerful manner as was expected of the ladies of the household. Her mother had set a precedent, and told her daughters that no matter how weary or heart sore a lady was she must always think of those around her and try to lighten their hearts, and think nothing of the affliction of her own.

"Kindness is a reward in itself," she frequently said. "Think of how good you feel when you say a word that brings a smile to the face of someone who is downcast, or ill, or discouraged because a cherished dream has been shattered or their heart suddenly broken."

Rachel had received this advice with a coy smile, but Leah had taken it to heart, and never forgot it. Instead of storing it away for future use, she put it into practice daily, no matter what her mood. Therefore, she did her best to present a smiling face to the world, even when the smiles were an effort and she was the one in need of comfort and encouragement.

Tonight, however, the sound of her father's braying laugh jarred on her nerves as she struggled with an aching head. A pain at her temple that shot up into the right side made her head throb and his laughter only served to intensify it. As soon as she could politely excuse herself she rose from the table and sat a little apart, allowing the gentle evening breeze to cool the fire that flushed her cheeks.

She closed her eyes and leaned back against the adobe wall of the upper porch of the house where the family liked to take their meals. The house was circular and resembled a bee hive, being cast in golden stone that glowed when the sun was reflected upon it. The many windows allowed a breeze to circulate and bring relief from the stifling heat.

Leah soon relaxed and the voices of those at the table seemed to come from a distance, sounding like the murmur of leaves on the trees sighing in the breeze of a June day, or the humming of bees droning around a hive on a lazy summer afternoon. She found the sound soothing and began to unwind and relax, sighing in contentment despite the pain in her head.

The sun began to sink below the horizon and the shadows of night came upon them. All around her the night sounds began and wove a spell of enchantment that held her in its gossamer clasp; crickets chirping their mesmerizing songs, the distant howl of a jackal, the plaintive cry of a nightjar winging its way through the air.

A smile lit her face and the pain in her temple began to ebb away. How she loved the song of the night! It had enthralled her, even as a small child, and never had its enchantment palled upon her. She allowed it to wash over her and carry her away from the mundane routine of everyday life and take her to a world that lay hidden from her gaze; mysterious, exciting, and beckoning her to enter into another realm...

She suddenly heard a rustling sound near at hand and opened her eyes to discover that she was not alone.

Jacob had come to sit beside her, and waited patiently for her to become aware of his presence. She blinked her eyes as if coming back home from a long journey, or emerging from a heavy sleep. They exchanged a fond smile and sat for a while as they listened together to the night in quiet contentment.

Often over the years Jacob had drifted into a habit of seeking her out to talk.

Leah was like a sister to him, he said, and he enjoyed her intelligent conversation and gentle humor, and appreciated her kindness and ability to encourage others.

On this night they sat in silence for some time, as the others drifted about them, Laban relating some interminable story of besting someone in the marketplace as Rachel giggled in amusement while the servants stood in attendance to anticipate their desires.

Finally Jacob spoke.

"A lovely night, is it not?" he said as he sighed and smiled at the stars, now glimmering in the expanse above.

Leah smiled as well, and found her gaze drawn upward. The indigo hue of evening had now deepened and the shadows of night had fallen. How vast was the heavens overhead, and how coolly the stars shimmered in that velvety blackness! Was there any other sight as lovely?

"Yes, indeed it is," she murmured softly in appreciation of the glory of the glittering expanse above.

They were silent once more as they contemplated the sky with its brilliant display. Suddenly Jacob began to count them. When he reached one hundred he laughed and turned to Leah.

"Forgive me, cousin, but I was suddenly struck by something my grandfather once told me, and I saw the humor of it," he remarked.

Leah turned a questioning gaze upon him with a smile about her lips that invited him to tell her more.

She enjoyed talking with Jacob and he had told her much of his family and the special destiny that they believed they had been given by their God, the God Who is never Named.

Many years ago his grandfather Abram had been called by his God from Ur in the land called the Fertile Crescent, said by some to be the very birthplace of civilization, where he had dwelt in ease and comfort. But there was another plan in the mind of his Deity, and he and his wife Sarai were instructed to leave Ur and follow God to a place that He had not yet revealed. They had obeyed and were led to the land of Haran, where they had settled for a time, ultimately leaving Abram's father there to spend the remainder of his days, while they packed up their belongings and moved on in obedience to God, as He led them further to their destination.

They had journeyed on and settled in the land of Canaan, a land that was rich and plentiful where he could raise his flocks and enjoy abundance. But there was one thing that Abram and Sarai lacked to make their joy complete; a son to carry on their legacy.

Abram was old and Sarai was barren, but God had made a promise to them to give them a son of their very own. Sarai laughed but Abram believed the word of his God. They waited many years without any sign of fulfillment of the promise, and in the waiting Sarai grew tired and suggested that Abram take her maid Hagar to his bed and their child would be counted as hers. The suggestion sounded logical to Abram, and he agreed, and when his son Ishmael was born it was a day of joy for him.

But Sarai had not foreseen how her heart would be devoured with jealousy, especially when the promise was eventually fulfilled and she bore Isaac to Abram in their old age. As Isaac grew his brother Ishmael and his mother who had been Sarai's maid mocked him, and she cast Hagar out of the house. Hagar and Ishmael had been met in the wilderness by the God Who was never Named, as He heard the cries of the lad, and being the God of mercy that He was, He promised to make a great nation out of the descendants of Ishmael as well.

Abram's name was changed to Abraham, for he was to be the father of many nations, and Sarai was christened Sarah, which meant princess. But Isaac was their only child.

When he grew into a young man his father did not wish him to take a bride from the pagan Canaanites around them, and so he sent his servant to the city of his brother Nahor, and instructed him to choose a bride from his family.

It was great fortune that Rebekah, the great-niece of Abraham, agreed to leave her family and travel with the servant to the land of Canaan to marry Isaac.

She quickly found favor with her new husband, who found comfort with her following the death of his mother, with whom he had shared a deep bond.

And to them were born the twins, Esau and Jacob.

Leah recalled all of this as she now waited for Jacob to reveal the source of his amusement.

She raised an eyebrow invitingly, and he smiled and continued.

"My grandfather once said that before my father was born, his God, the God Who is never Named, Who was also called the Lord, promised him that even as the stars were in the sky, so to would his descendants be; that is, too numerous to count."

Jacob chuckled and Leah joined appreciatively in his laughter.

"And how many descendants does he have?" she asked, knowing full well what the answer was.

"Just myself and my brother Esau," he laughed.

"Then I suggest that you both get busy populating the heavens," Leah advised him with all apparent seriousness even as she shook with sudden and uncontainable mirth.

They glanced quickly at one another and suddenly exploded into laugher with such intensity that it attracted the notice of Laban,

Adinah, and Rachel, who were startled by the sound and its source. Laban saw his daughter's betrothed being amused by her sister and a frown creased his brow. But Rachel's eyes flashed and her full lips tightened into a hard line as she rose from the table and headed toward her intended and her sister.

"Tell us what is so amusing," she spat out in a hard little voice.

Jacob started and stared at her in amazement. He had never heard her speak in any but the dulcet tones of the coo of a dove. His body tensed as he peered at her through narrowed lids as he examined her face intently.

Rachel suddenly relaxed her mouth and laughed, causing the tension to go out of Jacob's body and Leah to breathe easier. For she knew the moment she saw her sister's frown that a storm of temper could erupt without warning and she had no desire to be a target in its path, lest the havoc it wrought bring destruction upon herself.

But unknown to herself, the sight of she and Jacob enjoying one another's company had planted a seed in her father's mind that would soon bear bitter fruit.

Chapter 5
The Deception

The day had finally arrived, after seven long years of waiting. The spring air rang with the music of birdsong, the breezes gently wafted through the budding trees, and the days slowly grew longer.

It was time for the wedding of Jacob and Rachel.

It had not been easy to get Laban to set the date. The seven years had passed a few months before, but the wily older man refused to bring up the wedding or the termination of his nephew's servitude. He had made a great profit from the free labor that Jacob had given him, and his pastures filled with the fattening lambs and goats that frolicked in the fields.

At last after several hints to his uncle Jacob could bear it no longer and took it upon himself to force the issue.

"My seven years of servitude are completed, Laban," he said in the voice of utmost respect in which a hint of impatience strived to be contained. "Let me have my wife for whom I have slaved for you; for I am eager for her, and she is ready to be married."

Laban lifted an eyebrow and glanced with amusement at the impetuous young man who stood before him. It was true that his daughter was ready, for Rachel was now twenty-one, and most maidens were married by the age of fourteen. But the offer of free labor was so tempting that when Jacob made the offer to serve seven years for her he could not refuse it.

He speculated on what it would cost him to let Jacob go and hire another hand, and a frown creased his forehead as he thought of the additional expense on his purse. It would be costly; indeed it would. And the thought that occasionally visited him made its presence known once more...

But he shook his head inwardly as he outwardly wreathed his face in a smile of avuncular jocularity as he beheld the fervor of his love-struck nephew.

"Indeed, they are completed, and my daughter is ready," he smiled as he thumped Jacob on the shoulders with one of his beefy hands. "Just set the date and I will arrange everything to your satisfaction, and prepare a hearty feast in celebration of your union."

And the smile that radiated from his face originated not in the happiness of a good heart that wished others well and shared in their joy, but in the greed that lurked in the depths of his soul.

The guests had all assembled and taken their places. The smell of rich and spicy food was enticing as it drifted to their nostrils on the evening breeze. It was said that the wedding dinner was to consist of roasted lamb sprinkled with rosemary, and vegetables simmered in herbs brought from foreign lands, and the wine was imported from the finest vineyards; all to be served on the finest dishes that the house of Laban possessed.

Hangings of fine linen in crimson and blue draped the doorframe of the house as a symbol of celebration. Musicians played on the flute and drum as the guests began tapping their feet to the rhythm, and anticipated the dancing after the ceremony was completed. Many eyes turned to the doorway from which the bride would eventually emerge to leave her family and be joined to her husband.

A murmur of anticipation rang through the assembly.

How beautiful Rachel would look! True, one would not be able to see her through the heavy veil that in tradition swathed all brides as an outward mark of inward modesty; but her form would still be discernible and her robes should be of the finest quality, or so it was rumored, and knowing the pride of Laban, certain to be true. Such a man as he would never permit his daughter to be adorned in any but the finest garment money could buy on the most important day of her life.

The sound of flutes lilted as the signal for the guests to seat themselves and await the advent of the bride. The chatter died down to a polite murmur, which quickly faded and died away altogether. As they turned to face the porch and watch the doorway some noticed the absence of the bride's sister and speculated on the reason for it.

Poor Leah, one person whispered, forced to watch her younger sister be the first to marry. Perhaps it was too much to bear and she simply could not face it. Several heads nodded in agreement and pitied the poor disfigured maiden who would never know the joy of marriage or the pride of motherhood.

Or her father, being the proud man that he is, didn't want his daughter's reproach to be evident on the happiest day of her sister's life and he hid Leah away for his own sake, murmured another. After all, the older daughter usually marries first, and Leah had no prospects at all. And say what you will, Laban was no doubt ashamed of her appearance that would detract from his younger daughter's special day.

"Well, I am only glad that it is not my daughter who is afflicted in such a manner," said one lady who fanned herself with a palm leaf as she smugly arranged the folds of her robe so as not to wrinkle them.

"I completely agree," whispered another that sat nearby. "If my daughter was disfigured I would send her away. No doubt that is what Laban has done. He has secreted Leah away until the festivities are over."

"Yes," a rotund man in a fine robe agreed. "He does not wish to be reproached at having the younger girl marry before the older one. It is a shame on his pride that he cannot find a husband for Leah."

They nodded their heads and congratulated themselves that they were not cursed with such a daughter when there was a rustling noise heard in the doorway and several people turned and craned their heads in that direction to see the cause of the disturbance.

"Shhh!" someone admonished the whisperers, "here she comes!"

And there was the bride, standing in the

doorway clothed in dazzling white linen. Her heavy veil hid her features from view, but she moved with grace and dignity through the doorway, onto the porch, and down the steps to the midst of the assembled guests.

Many nudged their neighbor in the ribs at the look on the bridegroom's face. Why the young man was actually in tears! How romantic! But then again, this young Jacob seemed to be passionately in love with Rachel, even offering to serve her father seven years to obtain her hand; which indicated either a deep and abiding love for his bride or a profound and crippling stupidity that was exploited by the greed of his future father-in-law, depending on how you looked at it.

For who in their right man would actually trust a man like Laban to keep his word?

The sun rose and cast a dazzling ray of light into the bridal chamber, gradually illuminating it and revealing the occupants. It had been in darkness the night before with no lamp to light it, as was the custom in Haran. Such was to protect the modesty of the bride, the inhabitants said, and therefore all newly married couples faithfully adhered to the tradition.

The bride woke out of sleep first and gazed at the sight of her beloved, who lay in sleep sprawled across her. She sighed in deep contentment and stroked his hair, those thick waves and curls that she had always longed to run her fingers through! She blushed as she recalled the night just passed, and how tender and passionate Jacob had been. And in that night she had given her heart away and would never be able to take it back...

At last Jacob stirred and lifted his head. He did not open his eyes, but nestled his face down into the neck of his bride, kissing her throat and murmuring endearments. She closed her eyes in bliss, knowing this moment could not last, yet savoring it for as long as it did.

Finally Jacob sighed and rubbed the sleep from his eyes. He yawned and blinked his eyes open, and then lifted his head to gaze with rapture on the face of his sweetheart.

He gasped, his breath strangled in his throat; he blinked his eyes and shook his head as the color drained from his face. Although his mouth flew open, the power of speech forsook him momentarily. Shock widened his eyes as the full implication of his situation was borne home to him.

"Leah!" he shrieked. "What are you doing in my bed? Where is Rachel?"

Leah flinched and turned pale, biting her lip in anticipation of the storm to come. The moment of reckoning had arrived.

"She is not here, Jacob," she said faintly.

"What, what did you do with her?" he stammered, still not fully aware of what had happened.

"She was never here," Leah explained in a voice that was almost inaudible, her heart beating so rapidly that she feared she would faint.

She froze and could say no more, and held her breath as she waited for the explosion that was sure to follow.

Jacob stared at her, and was so still that it frightened her. Then he slowly shook his head from side to side and withdrew from her. He backed away from her and rose to his feet, oblivious of the fact that he was naked.

After several moments of staring at her with unseeing eyes, he spoke.

"Surely, you can not mean,..." he began, before losing his voice, "it can not be that you, that I...I...that is to say..."

Finally, able to bear it no longer, Leah said it for him.

"Yes, Jacob, it is true!" she shrieked, aghast at the sight of his aversion. "Rachel was never here. She was never in this bed. It is you and I that were married last night; not you and Rachel."

She would never forget the way that Jacob stumbled away from her, so dazed that he nearly left the bridal chamber without first donning his clothes. She gently pointed out his state, and at last he roused from his stupor as he vented his outrage.

"Get away from me! Don't touch me: I can dress myself!" he shouted, as he grabbed a robe and sped out of the room, stumbling as he ran.

Laban had planned his action well. In exchange for Rachel, Jacob was to work another seven years for her hand, but could marry her at the end of Leah's bridal week. He had been impervious to Jacob's plight and impassive when the young man confronted him.

"You tricked me!" Jacob had exclaimed. "I served you faithfully and you deliberately gave me the wrong bride. How could you do that to me?"

His pain and anger finally penetrated the few shrunken remnants of human feeling left in the old man's heart and he relented.

"It is not our custom to marry the younger daughter before the older one is wed," he stated, improvising a hasty lie.

It was true that traditionally the older married first, but that did not prevent the marriage of the younger one if a desirable party asked for her hand. Laban, however, thought it best not to enlighten his nephew on that fact, and presented to him only what he wished him to know and accept.

"And when I saw how much you and Leah seemed to enjoy talking and laughing with one another I thought that perhaps you might enjoy two brides instead of one. And think of what a reflection of your manhood that would be!"

Laban smiled from ear to ear with a wicked gleam in his eyes. Jacob glared at his uncle, with steam erupting from his own ears. He struggled within himself, longing to strike the wily older man who had robbed him of his joy and inflicted a new burden upon him in the addition of a second wife that he did not want; but he managed with great effort to conquer his rage and control his behavior. It was sad, but true, that this man held his fate in his hands...

And in the end, there was nothing he could to do change Laban's mind. So he obeyed his instructions and completed Leah's bridal week.

Knowing that he would soon have Rachel seemed to resign Jacob to his fate. After all, it was not uncommon for a man to have more than one wife, but usually they were of his own choosing. He initially resented Leah for going along with the deception, but eventually came to see that she simply obeyed her father as a good daughter is brought up to do. He therefore completed his duty to her and visited her every night.

As they lay together that week Jacob fell back into his old habit of confiding in her, and one night he found himself sharing with her a thought that came to his mind after he had discovered Laban's ruse.

"It may be my punishment," he said, rather tactlessly, as Leah turned wounded eyes upon him.

"I mean, for what I did to another," he hastened to say, not being able to bear the hurt he had carelessly inflicted upon her. "My people believe that the deeds of a man's hands return to him, and so mine may have returned to me."

He stroked her thick shiny hair and she relaxed and snuggled against him. She seemed content and he went on with his explanation.

"Do you know why I came to your father's house?" he asked her, as he kissed her brow in tender apology for his unwitting cruelty.

"No; you never said why," Leah rejoined, now surprised as she realized suddenly that Jacob had never revealed what drove him from his father's home to the house of her father.

"Well, it is because of what I did to my own brother, Esau," he began.

He faltered a moment, and hesitated, but decided to continue.

"We never were close, being so different, indeed, completely opposite in nearly every way," he explained. "In fact, I have often been told that we fought for supremacy in the womb and tormented my poor mother. She inquired of God and was told that two nations struggled in her womb and that the elder would serve the younger. It was to that prophecy that your father referred the day I arrived and that made me uncomfortable.

"And as we grew up the rivalry only intensified. You see, our father preferred Esau, because he is fearless and strong and loves to hunt. My father is fond of game and enjoyed the meat that my brother brought to him. My mother preferred me and I enjoyed spending time listening to the tales of our people, and the promise that God Who is never Named made to my grandparents.

"My grandfather had sent his servant to his homeland to take a bride from his people for my father because he did not want him to marry a pagan from the land of Canaan. So adamant was my grandfather that he made the servant swear a solemn oath that he would not take a bride from the Canaanites. And so the servant journeyed to Haran and brought back my mother Rebekah.

"But Esau provoked our parents and married two sisters of Canaan, who delighted in flaunting their idolatry before our mother. Our people dwell in tents, but they made Esau build them a fine house for them to live in, a fact that made him unpopular in the eyes of our people. Our mother bore with their insolence patiently, but they would not relent, and refused to show honor to her or our father. It became an unbearable situation, and finally one day I had what I thought was an opportunity to set things right.

"Esau came in from a hard day of hunting that left him weary and famished. I had just made a savory stew for the evening meal, and he insisted that I give him some. I was suddenly dazzled as I saw how I could profit from his hunger and weariness and set right a situation that had gone very wrong. And so I said to him, 'First, sell me your birthright.'

"He revealed how much he despised his birthright by agreeing without hesitation to sell it to me at once. He asked what good his birthright was to him when he was about to die of hunger. And so he sold me his birthright, and I was content with that.

"But a day came not long after this incident when our father told Esau to bring him game and dress it and make a fine meal, and then he would bless him. My mother heard it and hastened to tell me, and ordered me to kill a goat and dress it and make a fine meal of it and to take it to my father before Esau returned and pretend to be him, so that I might receive the blessing instead.

"I was frightened for Esau is hairy and I am smooth, and I knew my father would not be fooled by our deception, and I shuddered at his wrath were he to discover how we had tricked him. So my mother suggested that I wear Esau's clothing which bore the smell of game and place wool over my hands and forearms and at the nape of my neck so that I would seem hairy as my brother is. You see, my father was going blind and it was possible that the ruse just might succeed in fooling him.

"It did succeed, and he blessed me rather than Esau, with a blessing that gave me great power and prosperity for myself and the generations that would follow me. However, no sooner were the words out of his mouth than Esau returned from the hunt and all was revealed.

"Esau begged my father to take the blessing back and bestow it on him as intended. But my father could not take back what was spoken; it was irrevocable and would stand forever. Such is the nature of a blessing, and also of a curse; once spoken it can not be revoked.

"Esau, however, was furious with an anger that knew no bounds. He was ready to murder me, and promised that as soon as our father died (for he was very old and likely to pass on at any time) that my life would be his and he would be avenged for my stealing first his birthright and then his blessing. The latter especially outraged him as I deceived our father to obtain it.

"It was this threat of murder that frightened our mother, who gave me money in secret and begged me to flee to her brother Laban before Esau could make good his threat.

Had she not done so I might very well not be alive today; for Esau says what he means, and I have no doubt that he would have killed me had I lingered in Canaan. I therefore owe my life to my mother and her quick thinking on my behalf."

Leah listened with tears of compassion in her eyes as she saw the pain in her husband's face as he remembered the events that precipitated his leaving his family and homeland. She was stunned at the recital of Jacob's trickery and deceit, but she did not censure or criticize him for his unbelievable behavior. Truly everyone had something in their past of which they were ashamed and strived to hide from those around them, did they not? Who was she to judge Jacob, when she had just deceived him, albeit at her father's bidding?

So she gently stroked the curl on his forehead, and murmured soothing words as she did so. Tears sprang to Jacob's eyes and a sob was quickly stifled in his throat, and he briefly laid his cheek against the palm of her hand. He turned his head and kissed it suddenly and then continued.

"And now, here I am at her brother's house, and he deceived me by pretending you were Rachel, even as I deceived my father by pretending I was my brother."

Chapter 6
The Rivalry

All too quickly the bridal week of Leah was finished. It had been a week of exhilaration such as she had never known or even hoped to experience. The conjugal time with Jacob had changed her feelings for him. Hitherto she had regarded him as a cousin of whom she was fond, and with whom she shared a friendship born out of kinship and understanding.

But the times of intimacy as man and wife had altered her view of him forever. And she realized that she had fallen in love with him, and fervently hoped that he had fallen for her as well. He was tender in his caresses, and when they were alone he seemed to have no other thought but for her. He seemed content when they were together and there was a new softness in his eyes when he looked at her.

She hoped, oh! how she hoped that his heart was completely hers.

That she would discover she was profoundly mistaken would all too soon be apparent.

Two weeks had passed since Leah and Jacob were married. He had been wed one week later to Rachel in an elaborate celebration and then secluded with her for her bridal week. They had now come out of their conjugal seclusion and the family had assembled for the evening meal for the first time since Leah's wedding.

She was shattered, and trying her best to

hide her broken heart.

One look at Jacob's face and the way he gazed steadfastly at Rachel proved that her own hopes for his devoted love were dashed. His eyes never left Rachel's face; if she arose from the table his eyes followed her. Rachel smiled at him with an almost triumphant air, and at one point gave Leah a sidelong look to see whether her sister was watching.

Too late Leah remembered the storm of fury with which Rachel had reacted to Laban's unbelievable plan.

"Marry Jacob? Let Leah marry Jacob? How could you even *think* of doing this to me! He is *mine*! We have been betrothed for seven long years and waited all this time, never once complaining and always falling in line with your conditions, and now you want me to let him marry my sister? And after I have waited all this time?"

And the younger girl burst into a torrent of weeping, sobbing so vehemently that she soaked the sleeve of her robe with her tears and slapping away the hands of those who tried to comfort her.

"Listen to me, my child," Laban said in a rare soft voice, "you will still marry Jacob; have no fear of that! But this is an opportunity for your sister to be wed as well, for her to finally have a husband."

He had the decency to shoot an apologetic look at Leah, who did not appreciate the pity he felt for her. She swallowed hard, swallowing her pride as well as she did so. She would rather never marry at all than to submit to the deception her father wished her to take part in.

Did he not see how the three parties involved would suffer for years to come? Could he not understand the rivalry that must inevitably result from two sisters sharing a husband, vying for his time, and competing for his love? Or did he see it and simply did not care in his ambition to have his eldest daughter off of his hands?

Rachel now vented her fury on her sister with a savage intensity that left Leah reeling from the ferocity of it.

"This was *your* idea, no doubt," she snarled at Leah. "I have seen you over the years attempting to entice Jacob and take him away from me. Oh, yes you have; do not deny it! Yes, this was all *your* idea!"

Leah gasped, and for a moment could not breathe. She felt the room swirl around her and had to grasp the back of a chair to steady herself. The attack was so unfair.

"Sister!" she admonished Rachel. "That is not true! I would never do anything to hurt you, and I have never treated Jacob as anything other than my cousin. You know this!"

"Oh, I have seen the two of you talking together, laughing together! Secreted away together in a corner where you thought no one would see you!" Rachel shrieked. "*Always* you attempted to make him love you. I see it now; do not deny it!"

"No, that is not so! When have I ever done anything improper where Jacob is concerned? Never! We talked as friends and cousins and shared a sense of humor; that is all and nothing more. I swear it!"

Laban at this particular moment wisely saw the need to make peace if he wanted his plans to succeed. He was about to clumsily put his foot in his mouth once more when his wife entered the room. She quickly summed up the situation and attempted to intervene.

"Rachel, Rachel," she soothed as she scooped up her youngest daughter into her arms and rocked her like a baby while gently stroking her hair. "There, there! Hush, my lamb! All will work out, you shall see."

She crooned tenderly to her daughter in her sweet voice as she sang her softest lullabies, and Rachel's sobs rose to a crescendo at the tender touch of her mother's hand, and then subsided at last as she nestled in her mother's arms. Leah let out a deep sigh and sank to the mat on the floor at her feet as her strength suddenly deserted her. She sat with her arms around her knees, hiding her face and her shame from those present. Laban stood awkwardly, shifting his weight from one leg to another and hummed tunelessly as his wife shot him a reproachful glance.

Now Leah had to watch as her beloved husband clearly showed his preference for Rachel. Oh, she had always known that he loved her or he would not have served seven years of hard labor for her hand. She knew that full well and had been appalled at her father's plan, which the obedience of a daughter due her father forced her to comply with.

But Jacob's sweetness to her during her

own bridal week had opened a door of hope in her heart that she thought had been closed forever. How tenderly he had spoken to her, how much he had disclosed the secrets of his heart as he shared his family history with her night after night. She had basked in his caresses and luxuriated in his confidences, knowing that only to one that he trusted absolutely would he bare his soul as he had done with her. To no one did she reveal what he shared about his family and the deception that drove him away from his furious brother, lest he risk death at his hands.

She looked at the radiant beauty of her sister and how it dazzled Jacob, and wished in vain yet again that she had not been disfigured. Since Jacob had married Rachel, he appeared to have forgotten her existence. Everything that had happened between them during her own bridal week had apparently meant nothing to him. With a sudden flash of insight she realized with a pang that he had shown her nothing more than the momentary tenderness of a man enjoying his wife's embrace and caresses, but he did not love her as he so clearly did her sister.

And she did not know what to expect in their unusual marital arrangement. Would she and Rachel be expected to share Jacob? Or would he neglect her for Rachel now that he had the one he had always wanted?

With the passing weeks Leah's questions were answered. Night after night she was left alone and spent many sleepless hours tormented by loneliness and jealousy as Jacob abandoned her for her sister.

Bitter tears were her bedfellows as she wept for the rejection she felt in her heart. She should have realized that winning the love of Jacob was too much to hope for. He wanted another, had always wanted that other, and that was that. To hope otherwise was foolish indeed.

With that knowledge a furious rage rose up within Leah. How dare he use her for his own momentary pleasure and then cast her aside like this! He had caressed her, whispered endearments, and stroked her hair lovingly, only to abandon her when he finally received his heart's desire.

How cruel, how wicked to treat her so! Did he not know how she loved him, and how she longed to make him happy? Did he not care for her at all?

Even when he was betrothed to Rachel he had always had a kind word for her, had spent time talking to her when all other men ignored her and avoided looking at her. Jacob alone had shown her kindness and extended the hand of friendship. Now that was forgotten, no! it was ruined, she saw suddenly, by the marriage that had been forced upon them.

For she knew without a doubt that Rachel would find that friendship a threat now that she and her sister were both married to the same man. For if Jacob sought her out for companionship now it could lead to more than mere talk, as he might relapse back into the behavior of his bridal week with Leah, and Leah knew her sister would never permit that to happen. She sensed that Rachel would put every obstacle possible in the way of any marital relations between her and Jacob.

But as matters stood, the truth was that Rachel would not have to try very hard to prevent Jacob from seeking out Leah at all.

Many were the tears that Leah wept in the weeks to come. She was tormented by mental images of her husband her sister together and at times wished for death. How cruel to finally marry only to have her husband forsake her for another! The shame and indignity was more than she could bear, let alone the heartbreak in loving someone who didn't truly want her.

If it had not been for her mother she did not think she could have borne it. Adinah counseled her with wisdom gained through many trials, and advised her to wait and hope.

It was not an easy situation for anyone, her mother said, and probably for Jacob least of all.

This statement startled Leah out of her misery.

"Why would Jacob suffer the most?" she asked in astonishment. "He has his pick and choose of which wife he wants at the moment, while Rachel and I must wait for his favor and the bestowal of his company."

Adinah shook her head.

"No, daughter; he must be careful not to hurt either of you. If he spends time with you then Rachel is angry. If he neglects you, then you are hurt. If he shows affection to you, then you may believe he loves you more than he really does. And Jacob does love you, Leah; but it is not the same love that he has for Rachel. You do understand that, don't you?"

Leah snorted her disgust, amazed that her mother would even feel the need to make her aware of a fact that she knew entirely too well.

"Oh, I understand that far better than you think, Mother!" she exclaimed. "How many nights have I lain sleepless waiting for him to come, only to realize that he is with my sister instead?"

And she burst into a storm of bitter tears, despite her attempt to stifle them. They poured unheeding down her cheeks, wetting her upper lip with a salty taste as the sobs tore at her throat, and racked her body.

Adinah stroked her daughter's cheek and lifted her chin. Leah was forced to look at her mother, and cast sullen eyes upon her.

"You do not understand," Adinah said. "The love that Jacob has for Rachel is that of a beautiful woman that he desires. But it is you that he has given his heart to, my daughter. He just does not know it yet."

Leah gasped. She thought that her mother must have taken leave of her senses, so outrageous was the statement that had just fallen from her lips.

"What! That is not possible; he has abandoned me for my sister while I spend night after night alone. This is not the act of a man who has given his heart to a woman, to forsake her for another."

Adinah shook her head.

"Leah, you and Jacob have always been friends. With you he shares his thoughts and beliefs. A man does not do that with a woman unless there is a deep affection, a kindred spirit. And he did not cast you away when he knew that you were party to your father's deception, or abandon you when he knew he would still have Rachel as a bride. He completed his week with you, as is proper and right.

"But mark my words; a day will come when he will see that you are the one he was meant to be with, and not Rachel. And when that day comes his heart will be completely yours."

Chapter 7
The Firstborn

Over the next couple of months Leah's misery increased as she was forced to witness her sister's joy and endure her husband's avoidance of her. Lonely were her days and endless were her nights spent alone, waiting in vain for a husband who did not come to her. The world seemed a black place in which to dwell and she contemplated leaving it, although it was considered a serious offense to take one's life.

But unexpectedly everything changed in a single day.

Leah discovered that she was expecting a child.

At first she was astonished. She thought she must be mistaken, and said nothing until she was absolutely certain. She felt conflicting emotions; joy, fear, even shame and embarrassment, in view of the light of her husband's continued indifference.

Leah could not imagine how she would break the news to Jacob. The very thought made her stomach queasy and her breath fail her. How would he react? Would he be pleased? Or would he be merely annoyed, wishing that it was his favorite wife who would bear his firstborn instead of the one that had been forced upon him through the trickery of her father?

She confided in her mother before planning a course of action.

"Oh, Leah, this is wonderful!" Adinah exulted. "How delighted I am; my first grandchild! I can not wait for it to come into the world."

And Adinah wiped a tear of joy from her eye and patted her daughter's shoulder. Leah moaned and buried her face on her mother's shoulder and gave way to a shower of sobs.

"There, there, child," Adinah soothed, "there is no cause for weeping! It is happy news that you have shared!"

"But, Mother, you do not understand!" Leah wept. "Jacob will probably not be pleased with the news. And Rachel will be furious that it is I who will give him his firstborn and not her."

Adinah sobered at this last statement. She knew in her heart that Leah had indeed spoken the truth, and that her sister would be furious that Leah carried Jacob's child.

Leah mustered all of the courage that she possessed. Over and over in her mind she rehearsed what she would say to Jacob to announce her impending motherhood, and the arrival of his firstborn. No scenario played satisfactorily in her mind, however, and she finally resolved to just speak to him and allow the words to come naturally and unrehearsed. She forsook her wounded pride and steeled herself to seek out Jacob.

He had avoided her since he married Rachel, not even looking her in the eye. The family meals were uncomfortable for all of them, with Leah looking downcast, Jacob avoiding her gaze, and Rachel glaring at her sister. Now the news she was about to impart to him would make those already uncomfortable meals completely intolerable.

She made no attempt to seek him out when she knew that her sister would be around, but instead went to Jacob during the day when she knew he would be working for her father. At the moment he was engaged in digging a canal that would be used for irrigation, bringing water from a nearby stream to water their crops and to provide drinking water for themselves and their livestock.

When he heard Leah approach, Jacob lifted his head to see who ventured near, then ducked his head and gave his full attention to his task. Leah's courage failed her for a moment when she saw his behavior, and her legs buckled beneath her. She nearly turned around to go back to the house, but she had no choice other than to proceed.

"Hello, Jacob," she said softly in a voice that was barely above a whisper. "You appear to be hard at work. I hope the day is not too hot for you."

"Hello, Leah," Jacob said without raising his eyes. "If it is hot it is to be expected; it is July, after all."

He kept his gaze doggedly on the canal he was digging, and did not glance again in her direction.

"But no, it is not too hot for me," he replied without lifting his head.

The awkward silence that followed might have lasted forever had Leah not been forced to impart her news. After all, a man had to know that he had a child on the way. At some point she had to tell him, and the sooner the better.

She took a deep breath and then slowly exhaled it. She clenched her fists and strengthened her spine, standing to her full height. At last she plunged in.

"Jacob; I have some news for you. Something I must tell you."

The words tumbled from her lips even as her mouth went dry. She finally had his reluctant attention. He gave her a sidelong glance from beneath his thick lashes.

"What is it?" he asked, as he kept digging.

She floundered, not knowing how to proceed. It occurred to her that there was only one bit of news that a wife could ever give to a husband, and he should sense that. And she was visited by a sudden inspiration. If Jacob did not realize what that news was, then he had never truly been her husband, had never felt any true tenderness for her, but had only used her for his pleasure as a man would use a concubine.

Finally she spoke and her heart pounded as she hoped that he would guess her news...

"Can you not guess what it is?" she asked softly.

For a very long moment there was absolute silence. It was so still that Leah could hear the rustle of the grass as a breeze gently ruffled it, and the drone of a bee that buzzed nearby. A bead of sweat formed above her upper lip and she tasted its salty tang as she licked her dry lips.

And then Jacob abruptly stopped digging and slowly rose to his full height to face her. He looked her full in the face, and his eyes widened as he gazed into her eyes. His breath caught in his throat, and he sucked air in through his teeth.

"Do you mean..." he began, and stopped to inquire of her eyes.

There he found the answer, and he swallowed hard. He gasped and shook his head as if to clear cobwebs away. He stood in silence, staring at her, and then the realization was borne home to him.

"I am going to be a father!" he exclaimed. "Truly? Me? A father!"

He buried his face in his hands and then wiped his face with them. Jacob glanced up at the heavens and a sob escaped his throat. Leah watched him, hardly daring to breathe, so great was her anxiety.

Jacob turned to her, and seeing her fearful face, suddenly grabbed her and clutched her tightly to his chest.

In the months that followed Leah became the most important member of the household. All were careful to make her comfortable and satisfy her every whim, hoping that by doing so it calmed her temperament and ensured an easy delivery when the child was born.

All that is, except Rachel.

She did not voice aloud her anger and jealousy that her sister should be the first to bear a child, nor her pain that her husband had fathered a child with any other woman, let alone her own sister. But many were the times when she was seen biting her lips at some innocent remark carelessly uttered by Laban and Adinah, both so proud of Leah and their excitement at the impending arrival of their first grandchild. And all it took was the sight of her sister's increasing girth or the joy in Jacob's face when his eyes fell upon Leah to make Rachel clench her fists tightly at her side.

Her bitterness was plain to everyone, and many glances were turned away from her as they witnessed the anger she harbored against her sister. Even Jacob avoided her gaze, and Leah felt pangs of guilt every time she saw Rachel and felt her unspoken resentment.

Still, it was gratifying to be the object of Jacob's devotion. He lavished care and concern upon Leah and spent his nights with her, talking as they once had, and musing on the child to come. As the child grew in her womb, he placed a hand upon her stomach to feel the baby kicking, and laughed in delight at the strength of the impact.

"It will be a boy; I can tell," he chortled. "A son! What a miracle! What a blessing from the Lord!"

Leah alone knew what leaving his family behind had cost Jacob. A son would fill the empty void in his heart. And Leah savored those moments of joyful expectation with him, and hoped that his devotion would last.

The sound of the plaintive cry pierced through the excruciating pain that seemed to engulf her entire body. She lay in a daze, exhausted from the hours of labor that felt like an eternity, without beginning or end. It was as if she had been in labor forever and would go on so, pushing and crying out at the relentless pain. At last it was over and the child presented.

It was a boy; a perfectly formed son, who already showed evidence of possessing his father's dark wavy hair and wide dark eyes framed by thick lashes. He flailed about him, punching the air with his little fists until he was given to his mother, who hastened to nurse him.

Jacob sat with her, lifting a tiny hand to examine the fingers, which clutched about his hand in a tight grip that would not let go. His father laughed and kissed the top of his head exuberantly. Then he turned to Leah and kissed her cheek.

"Well done," he told her. "A son. Blessed is the Lord, the God Who is never Named!"

Leah joined in his exultation, and wept tears of joy. Despite her exhaustion, she felt that this was the happiest day of her life. A child of her own to love, and a son to fill his father's heart with pride. Perhaps now her husband would love her for herself.

She had been learning much from Jacob in the months they had shared awaiting the birth of this son about the God Who was never Named. It was to this God that she now prayed, she who had never truly believed in any deity.

But she felt that He had seen her in her suffering and loneliness and opened her womb to give Jacob his first child. And He had answered her prayers when she asked for a healthy child and a safe delivery of her son into the world, and so now she gave this God her devotion. She began to believe in her heart that the Lord had seen her affliction and He had given her a son so that she might win her husband's heart.

They had not decided on a name in all the months of waiting, both of them stunned that they had actually created a child between them, they who had been forced into a marriage that neither had ever sought. But now the perfect name for this child popped into Leah's head and she bestowed it immediately.

"I know just what we shall call him," she said to Jacob. "His name will be Reuben."

"Reuben," Jacob mused. "Yes, you are right. "A son."

And so Reuben he was called.

And outside on the porch, Rachel wept bitterly.

Chapter 8
The Family

Reuben was only the beginning.

The next few years were busy ones as the family grew. Leah proved to be fertile and she bore one child after another to Jacob. To her sorrow, however, she seemed no nearer to winning his heart after bearing him his firstborn son. Although he treated her with tenderness and delighted in each child that she bore him he never told her he loved her, never gazed with passion upon her.

Many were the tears of disappointment that she shed when she came upon him and Rachel one day in the field, locked in a passionate embrace, looking at one another with the same burning desire as they had during Rachel's bridal week.

Leah crept quietly away and they did not even know that she had seen.

Jacob fell into a pattern of spending one week with Rachel, and then a week with Leah. It proved to be the only way to keep peace between them. If he spent more time with one than the other then he must face wounded glances from Leah and a spate of fury from Rachel. And in his heart, he did not know which was worse.

It was as if he danced with rotating partners who competed for his attentions and demanded his affections, all the while feeling that he was a prize whose favor was fought over and sought after like an oasis in a desert land.

After Reuben came Simeon, so named because Leah was convinced that the Lord had heard that she was unloved and had sent this child to comfort her. Indeed, when this child was born he turned his head around until he found his mother and let out a whimper that only ceased when she took him in her arms. As she kissed the rosy little cheek he nestled close, and Jacob slipped in next to them and put an arm around them both, and kissed first the top of Simeon's head, and then Leah's.

In truth, he seemed as delighted with the birth of this son as he had Reuben, and marveled aloud that the Lord had blessed him so greatly.

The year rolled around and Leah bore a third son to Jacob. She christened this one Levi, and fervently hoped that he would come to see that their union was blessed of the Lord, especially in light of the fact that Rachel had yet to conceive. How she longed for Jacob's love! With the birth of each child, she searched his eyes hungrily for the look that she craved, the one he bestowed upon her sister that seemed unaware of anyone else in the room.

She never found it there.

Leah was expecting again. This time she took little joy in the pending birth. She felt weary in her body. The boys had come so closely together, each one seeming more full of energy than the one before, and their care wore her out.

Her mother attempted to help when she could, but Adinah had stunned the family by starting to bear sons of her own. Three sons came in rapid succession and their vitality that they had inherited from their father took a toll on her advancing years. She delighted in them as much as Laban did, but keeping up with them was a challenge.

Nevertheless, both she and her husband marveled at the sight of them every day. In vain had she and Laban waited and prayed for sons, but all they had conceived were two daughters, which was not considered sufficient for one of Laban's status, and for one who sought the approval of men as he did. Now, however, they were blessed by the gods, Laban declared, because of the prosperity that Jacob had brought them.

Laban remembered very well the wealth that the servant of Abraham had displayed when he had come searching for a bride for Isaac, and Abraham had only grown in wealth and worldly goods since that time. It was said that he was especially blessed by his God, the God Who was never Named, for want of which Abraham and his family referred to as the Lord. They said that God's Name was so holy that it must never be uttered. And as He was the only God and Lord of all creation, that was how He was addressed.

Not that Laban himself bowed down to this God or addressed Him as the Lord. But he told Adinah that, nevertheless, Abraham's God had blessed him and his family and that this divine favor had passed down to Jacob. And because Jacob lived in his household all within prospered.

Why, just look at how many sons Leah

had borne, and so quickly too! And his own flocks; had they not multiplied and enjoyed good health? There was no disease to be named among them, and they grew strong and robust and brought good prices in the marketplace when he sold their wool. His stature had risen among his neighbors also; for the obvious health of his flocks meant that to buy a goat or a lamb from Laban ensured that the animal would live a long and healthy life.

And now, this blessing had extended to Laban's own family and Adinah had borne him three sons, as many as Leah had borne Jacob. And how pleased he was with his own little Beor, Alub, and Murash! The spitting image of their father they were, and how that made his heart swell with pride! Not that there was anything wrong with their mother's appearance, he hastened to assure Adinah, but a man did want his son to bear his image, after all.

Laban had also continued to utilize Jacob's labor. His second term of seven years had but three to go and he was reluctant to lose his favorite worker. He knew that when the seven years were up that Jacob would want to leave and find his own way in the world, which meant that he must go to the expense of replacing him, an undertaking that he did not desire at all.

He must find some way to keep Jacob firmly in his clutches, but how?

Leah had endured the months of confinement and would soon give birth to this fourth child. She had prayed daily for another son and for a safe delivery. And as she prayed, she found herself enveloped in a warmth that felt like a protective covering around her, giving her peace and contentment.

Was it the presence of the Lord? Had He put his arms about her when she prayed to Him? Despite her anxiety over her state of affairs, she found a new joy spring up within her, and felt that all would be well, regardless of how circumstances seemed, as she continued to vie with her sister for their husband's time and affection with such a ferocity that the two were rapidly becoming bitter rivals who desired nothing more than the defeat of the other.

Leah gave a mighty push and heaved so hard that the veins stood out in her neck. She was drenched in perspiration and felt her hair matted against the nape of her neck, and her robe was saturated, giving her a momentary chill due to its wetness. But she did the midwife's bidding and pushed again, this time bearing down hard.

The room spun around her and for a moment she felt so faint that she feared she would collapse. The midwife slapped her wrists and gripped her face in her hands, forcing her to look at her and focus. Leah snapped out of her faintness and gulped air into her lungs.

She inhaled deeply and pushed again as she gritted her teeth and clenched her fists against the pain. At last she was free of the burden and she felt her newest child enter the world. The reassuring sound of the baby's cry came to her ears and brought a smile to her weary face. She could at last lay back against the cushion and breathed deeply, gulping in the cool air of evening and closing her eyes in her exhaustion, ready to fall into a deep sleep.

But before she could do she heard the cry of her husband.

"Another son!" Jacob crowed, holding his latest up to the heavens, before kissing him soundly on the forehead.

Leah held out her arms and her baby was placed in them. Tears filled her eyes as she drank in the sight of him. No matter how many children she bore, she took delight in each one, and wondered anew at the miracle of each birth.

Jacob laughed suddenly and turned an amused glance upon Leah.

"Hmmm?" she asked faintly, tired from the birth yet curious about her husband's amusement.

"I just remembered something," Jacob answered and chuckled softly as he cradled his new son.

"What did you remember?" Leah asked.

Jacob straightened his spine and held the baby close as he looked at Leah.

"Do you remember telling me once that my brother and I had better start populating the heavens if we were going to have descendants that were like the stars, too numerous to be counted?" he asked.

Leah suddenly remembered and burst into giggles.

"And now here we are with four sons!" she exclaimed.

They laughed for a long moment together.

She wiped her eyes as she reflected that never had she expected that she would have a hand in bringing those descendants into the world, nor did Jacob, which was the cause of his amusement.

Then they turned their attention back to the baby.

"What shall we call him?" Jacob inquired.

"We shall name him Judah," Leah declared as a sudden inspiration flooded her.

Jacob glanced at her with a question in his eye. He raised an eyebrow and Leah laughed.

"Yes! Judah," she repeated. "Because I praise the Lord."

And she crooned over Judah a song of praise and thanksgiving to the Lord Who had unexpectedly blessed her with such incredible happiness.

Chapter 9
Rachel's Woe

Rachel's bitterness turned to anger against her husband. Surely it was Jacob's fault that she had no children; for had he not spent so much time with Leah that he had neglected her? It could not be her own fault, for had she not waited patiently for him all those years, spurning any other offer for her hand?

She reproached Jacob with this, and upbraided him for not giving her children.

"Give me children, just as you have my sister!" she demanded. "I am the one you love, not her. Where are the sons that I should have? Give them to me or I shall kill myself to escape my reproach of barrenness and your woeful neglect of me."

Jacob had never thought that he would ever feel anything but adoration and passion for his beloved, but now as he looked at her he was stunned by the jealousy of her sister that he saw on her face in the pursing of her lips, and the fury against him that blazed from her eyes. Indeed, he would not have been surprised to see smoke flaring from her nostrils, so great was her fury.

He recoiled from this evidence of his goddess' humanity and felt a surge of righteous anger sweep through him at being upbraided so unfairly by the one he had loved and worked for, enduring seven long years of hard labor that he might win her.

"Are you reproaching me for not giving you

children?" he asked her with incredulity in his eyes, as his voice rose in outrage.

His dark eyes snapped and Rachel suddenly became aware that she had roused his anger, something she had not thought possible so used was she to his slavish adoration, and she found herself taking an involuntary step backward, her palms raised outwardly.

But Jacob's anger was aroused and he did not back down.

"Am I in the place of God?" he asked her. "It is the Lord Who gives children; it is not in my power to do so. Were it possible, I would have given you many children, but we must bow to Him and to His will."

Rachel clamped her lips tightly together and tossed her head in the air. Indignation was evident in the way she held her head so high that the thought occurred to Jacob that if it had been raining she would have been in danger of drowning, so high were her nostrils in the air.

"You should think better of your attitude and humbly pray to the Lord to ask Him for children, and not blame me for not giving them to you," he advised.

Rachel whirled her head around and glared at him.

"Perhaps if you spent your nights with me and none with my sister I would have had children by now," she hissed with all the venom of a cobra about to strike.

Jacob was not pleased with her words or her attitude, and he stiffened as he faced her, his face suddenly wooden and set in bitter lines.

"Your sister is fruitful, and blessed of the

Lord. It pleases Him to give her children," Jacob informed Rachel.

He had one more thing to say on the matter, however, before he considered it closed.

"Just as it pleases me to receive them."

Jacob left her standing with a stunned and woebegone look on her lovely face.

Rachel was not accustomed to such treatment. All of her life her wishes were granted with alacrity and she had never been denied anything she desired. For the first time she saw that life had no guarantees, and that to wish for something was not to automatically have fulfillment of the desire.

She was too heartbroken for tears. She had shed as many as Leah, not for Jacob's love, which she took for granted, but for the reproach of childlessness to be removed from her. She knew that there was no greater shame for a married woman than to be barren. And she undoubtedly was.

But how could she conceive and so be able to hold up her head with dignity again?

The idea came to her in a burst of memory. She recalled a story that Leah had told her once, something that Jacob had shared with her about his family. For a moment her bitterness returned as she realized that Jacob never shared anything about his family with *her*, yet he freely did with Leah. Then she forced herself to calm down and quieted herself to better concentrate on how to make the memory work in her favor.

Leah had said that Jacob told her that when the Lord promised Abram a son, his wife Sarai had laughed as she was too old for childbearing. She therefore concluded that he had better take her maid Hagar to his bed and the child she bore on Sarai's knees would be counted as Sarai's since Hagar was her maid and therefore her property.

Rachel brooded on this for some time, and then slowly nodded her head.

Yes, she thought, that is how I shall do it.

She sought out Jacob at the first opportunity. He was in the fields once again and she made sure that she had donned the robe that he liked best to see her in; a garment of scarlet linen that contrasted vividly with her black hair and sparkling dark eyes. She wound a piece of scarlet linen about her head and allowed her mane of thick curls to dangle becomingly from it.

Her preparations were not in vain. Jacob looked up and smiled a slow smile that was full of promise as he savored the sight of her. She held out her hand and he kissed it, then drew her close to kiss her lips as well; a long kiss that seemed to drink from her lips like a thirsty man at a well of cold water.

When he finally released her she was breathless and wished there was some place where they could be alone. But they were in an open field for anyone to see...

Rachel could tell by the fire in Jacob's eyes that he had the same thought as she. But he was working for her father and could not be excused to satisfy his desire. So she contented herself with the certainty that he would visit her tonight and not Leah.

"You seem in a happier mood, Rachel," Jacob commented, as he adored her with his eyes. "What has brought about this change?"

Rachel smiled at him with the satisfaction that she had roused in him, exactly what she wished to do. Yes, tonight he would come to her...

"Oh, I thought about our conversation," she answered, and ran a hand over his muscular forearm. "And I agree that you are right, Jacob. Children are sent by the Lord."

Jacob's eyes widened. Rachel had never spoken like this before, and her statement took him by surprise.

"And?" he asked, holding his breath as he waited for her to continue.

"Well, I had an idea occur to me," she stammered, suddenly wondering if what she was about to suggest was truly the right course to take after all.

She hesitated for a moment, reconsidering; then the thought of Jacob with her sister and fathering her children roused her jealousy once again and strengthened her resolve.

"And my idea is this; your grandmother Sarai gave your grandfather Abram her maid Hagar to bear him a son that was counted as her own. I can give you my maid Bilhah. If she were to conceive by you, any children of hers will be counted as mine.

"I think that is a reasonable solution to

our problem, don't you?"

It was nine months later that Bilhah bore a strong son that Rachel joyfully christened Dan.

"Now, the Lord has vindicated me and given me a son," Rachel exulted as she took the child into her arms.

She held him triumphantly in her arms and gloated at her husband in the ecstasy of victory.

A second son came forth from Bilhah. This one Rachel named Naphtali.

"I have wrestled with my sister mightily, and I have prevailed!" she declared.

She did not notice the look of dismay that crossed her husband's face.

For the first time he did not delight in the births of his sons. He knew that many sons were a credit to a man as a reflection of his manhood, and that the more he sired the more use they would be in doing the work of his household. But he did not experience the joy he had felt when Leah brought forth her sons, conceived by him in the bond of marriage. This must be the cause of his lack of joy, he told himself.

Or was it the attitude he sensed from Rachel that these sons were merely a prize for her and a vindication for her continued barrenness, and that she felt no true desire to be a mother or to bless her husband with children from her womb out of a genuine love for him?

Jacob returned to Leah, appalled by

Rachel's attitude. But for the first time, although he and Leah spent much time in intimacy, she did not bear any children. This fact concerned Leah, as she believed it was the key to winning Jacob's heart. Before and after the birth of each son he had shown great tenderness for her, and she still hoped that the day came when it bloomed into true love and brought marital happiness.

She came up with the remedy her sister had used with such success.

"Here is my maid, Zilpah," she said to Jacob. "Take her and get sons from her and they shall be counted as mine."

From Zilpah came first Gad, for Leah declared herself fortunate at his birth; and then Asher, so named because his birth made her happy.

At this point Leah had given Jacob four sons of her own and two by her maid servant. With the two birthed by Rachel's maid Bilhah the count stood at eight in all. Many men would have been happy with half that number and Jacob counted himself blessed to have so many. Surely, their number was complete and he could not expect any more children from his wives.

But he would discover that he couldn't have been more wrong in his assumptions.

Chapter 10
Leah's Woe

The seasons came and the seasons went with unfailing regularity. Spring blossomed into summer, summer passed into autumn, autumn faded into winter, and winter melted into spring.

It was now the time of the wheat harvest and the fields were once more ripe and full. The sky overhead was as soft and blue as a robin's egg, and was dotted with clouds so white that they dazzled in their purity, and so fluffy that they made one long to lay one's head upon them as if they were the softest of pillows. The grass still wore the emerald sheen of May, not yet having taken on the dull and dreary look of July when the sun baked everything in its unrelenting heat.

June had always been a favorite month of Leah's. She loved the soft balmy breezes and the gentle swaying of the olive trees, the lengthening days and the increasing warmth. Everywhere she looked about her it seemed that life had burst forth and was celebrating in exuberant joy. The children were lively in their play, couples loving in their courtships, and the crops springing up seemingly overnight. The birds sang in the trees, and delighted the ears of all who listened, enchanting and lulling the heart with their lovely melodies, so varied and abundant, yet somehow blending together in sweet harmony.

Only she felt that life was dull and barely to be endured.

She had not borne a child in several years, which caused her some concern as she had shown such great fertility in the ability to bear children. Her other sons were shooting up like the golden wheat in the fields around her, and she delighted in them and daily blessed the Lord for the gift of them, still amazed at His goodness in providing them; but she wondered when they might have another brother or even a sister to join them.

Idly she reflected on them, these strong and vital sons of hers; Reuben, the firstborn, who was so volatile and passionate of feeling. He did not like to see his mother neglected and resented the sons born by the maids Zilpah and Bilhah. He was always courteous to them but cold and did not invite Gad or Asher to play with him or his younger brothers.

Simeon was sensitive and erupted in explosive anger at the slightest offense but was also quick to soothe his younger brothers, always desiring to set things right and bring justice for perceived wrongs. In this he was joined by his brother Levi, who vehemently agreed with whatever Simeon stated and abetted him in whatever he proposed to do. So alike were they in their convictions and temperament that Leah often jokingly said that they were twins who were born years apart although conceived at the same time.

Judah was her pride and delight, however, the one who prudently weighed his actions before implementing them, even though he was of tender years. This one had the mark of leadership on him, his mother reflected. It was a pity that he was born fourth in line, for it was evident to Leah that he would be the one who should inherit the mantle of his father, had it not been for the order of his birth.

The sons conceived by the maids received every bit as much attention from Leah as the ones she herself had borne. They were still Jacob's sons and therefore it was her duty to love them. She did not find this difficult, as children always managed to find their way into her heart, and they kept her on the run from morning until night. Indeed, so busy did all of the boys keep her with their active little lives and their desire to have her join in their frolics and soothe them in their fears that she collapsed into her bed at night, worn out from the time and energy she invested in them.

But she longed for more children, remembering the word Jacob had spoken that was given to Abram, that his descendants would be as the stars in the heavens, too numerous to count; and desired that the greater portion of those descendants should come from her own loins, and not those of her sister.

Jacob still paid her the marital visits regularly and continued to divide his time between her and Rachel, who had yet to conceive, an issue that grieved her bitterly. But Leah did not conceive either and it had begun to gnaw at her like a sore tooth that ached with a sharp and continuous pain.

Her mother tried to assure her that women often experienced these patterns of fruitfulness and barrenness. Why, just look at her for example; she had had only two daughters in the days of her youth, and then had three sons conceived out of the blue when she thought she was done with childbearing altogether! Leah had borne four strong and healthy sons in a very short time and her body needed rest, although she might not realize it. One day her womb would open again and she would be ripe with more children to bless her days.

Adinah neglected to tell Leah that she had already had a similar talk with Rachel, who mourned in deep sorrow over never having had any children at all.

The sound of piping voices startled Leah and she snapped out of her reverie as two of her sons ran into view and up to the porch where she sat looking out on the summer day as she sewed garments for her boys. The sight of the round face of Reuben with his sparkling brown eyes lit up with some secret delight brought a smile to her face and she laid down her sewing in preparation to sweep him up in her arms.

"Mother!" cried Reuben. "Look what I found in the wheat field; mandrakes. I picked them for you."

And the young boy proudly presented them to his mother as if they had been a bouquet of spring flowers with which to brighten the corners of a darkened room.

Mandrakes! Leah leaped up out of her seat and extended her hands eagerly to her son. At that very moment Rachel sprang around the corner. She had been somewhat listlessly taking a walk to have something to do and had returned just in time to hear Reuben's words.

"Mandrakes!" she exclaimed. "You found mandrakes? Where? Oh, what does that matter? Please give some of them to me!"

But Leah put up a hand at her sister, stemming the flow of her words. She accepted the mandrakes from her son, thanking him for his thoughtfulness, and patted him on the head, telling him and his brother Simeon, who had followed in his brother's wake to proudly present the gift of the mandrakes, to run along and find little Asher and tell him to come in for his nap. Reuben's eyes darkened and snapped at the mention of Asher's name, but Leah shot him a warning glance and he sullenly obeyed, muttering under his breath as he stomped away to do her bidding.

No sooner were the boys out of earshot then Rachel impatiently renewed her petition to her sister.

"Leah," she importuned with blazing eyes, "let me have some of those mandrakes."

Leah turned hard eyes on Rachel, and tightened her lips into a narrow line. She could hardly bear to look at her, standing there so sure and confident of herself, as she secretly despised her sister. Leah's long buried resentment that she had hidden for so long in an effort to preserve family unity finally flared up and she permitted herself the luxury of exploding and revealing her wounded feelings.

"Is it not enough that you have taken my husband?" the words erupted from her lips before she could stop them. "Now you want my son's mandrakes that he gave me as a gift, even demanding them from me? Is there no end to your greed, Rachel?"

Rachel blinked her eyes and sucked her breath through her lips as her eyes glittered at Leah.

"*Your* husband?" she sneered. "He was always intended to be *my* husband; and you stole him from me!"

Leah felt a strong urge to slap her sister, but managed to restrain herself. She felt her face grow hot as she shook with silent rage and clenched her fists so hard she felt her nails digging into her palms, drawing blood. Rachel saw her rage, however, and a smirk of satisfaction spread across her face like a monsoon cloud in a stormy sky.

"I had no choice in that matter," Leah said through her tightly clenched teeth. "You know this. Father made me do it."

"Oh, Father *made* you do it? Then why do you call him *your* husband?" Rachel challenged her. "You act as if he really *is* your husband, instead of someone that Father "forced" you to marry."

"I called him my husband because he *is* my husband!" Leah erupted at last, too far provoked in her anger to be prudent and show caution. "Perhaps you forget that it is *I* who have borne him children, and not you. Believe me, our marriage is not a mere pretense that is maintained for appearance's sake. We conceived those children together; they didn't just suddenly appear out of a clear blue sky."

Her words hit their target. Nothing she

could have said would have wounded her antagonist more deeply. Rachel flinched and put up a hand to a face gone suddenly pale. She moaned and bowed over as her sister's words pierced her heart.

Leah flinched momentarily; she wished she could feel compassion for her, but Rachel had caused her far too much pain. And yet she knew how her sister must feel at being barren. Was she herself not trying to have more children and wondering why her womb failed to produce? How much greater must be the pain of a woman who had borne no child at all...

Leah stood impassive, however, with the iron resolve of a woman in love, and offered no comfort to the shattered woman before her, as she waited for Rachel to compose herself. It took several moments for that feat to be accomplished. But finally Rachel straightened and stood erect and passed a hand over her eyes and looked with unseeing eyes at her sister.

"If you will let me have some of those mandrakes, I will let you take my turn and you can have Jacob tonight," she said in a dull and lifeless tone. "I will not interfere; I promise."

Leah wanted so much to be able to turn down the offer that was made to her. How it galled her that Rachel had favor with their husband to the extent that she could afford to miss a turn with him and it would not change Jacob's desire for her. Yet Leah knew in her heart that she herself would miss no opportunity to share the act of love with him.

But it did not soothe her wounded pride to realize that Rachel knew it.

When Jacob came in from the fields Leah met him wearing a robe of green linen and the amber beads he had presented her with after the birth of Reuben, when his heart had been swelled with such pride over his firstborn son that he wished to honor the woman who had borne him. She adorned her face with a smile and had dabbed some fragrant oil of sandalwood on her body. She held out her hands to Jacob and whispered in his ear.

"You will be coming to me tonight, because I have hired you for the evening. Rachel wished for some of the mandrakes that Reuben picked for me and I consented to let her have some. So tonight you are mine."

Leah knew why Rachel wanted the mandrakes so desperately and had demanded them of her sister. Some believed that they were a cure for barrenness; that they contained some hidden property that made the womb fruitful. She knew of several women in Haran who insisted that they conceived after eating them.

But they did not solve this problem for Rachel.

Instead, it was Leah who conceived. She thrilled at the thought of another child, and wept happy tears at its coming. Nine months later she gave birth to another son whom she named Issachar.

God has given me my reward because I gave my maid to my husband, she said in her heart. He has recompensed me for the pain of sharing my husband.

Jacob was evidently pleased with Leah for bearing yet another son to add to their growing family, because one year later she brought forth still another to add to their number. Zebulon was a plump baby with a delightful giggle that burst out whenever he was tickled; something his overjoyed father was pleased to do so that he might hear his son laugh and chuckle with him.

And Leah was confident that her husband would turn from her sister and live solely with her because she had given him six sons.

It was with great astonishment that a seventh child followed quickly on the heels of Zebulon; but for the first time a daughter was added to the family. Leah's heart felt a tender protectiveness of the tiny baby girl that was placed in her arms. The soft plaintive cry that emanated from the babe's lips clutched at her heart.

A daughter! Not considered as valuable as a son, but something she would treasure, nonetheless. She thought of her relationship with her own mother Adinah and the comfort her wisdom had given her all of her life. How she hoped for such a bond with this little girl who had just come to bless her!

And she could think of no other name to bestow on her than a diminutive of her own mother's, and the child was subsequently named Dinah.

Despite her careful machinations the mandrakes had failed her, and Rachel was in the depths of despair, not knowing where to turn next. It was more than she could bear to watch her sister deliver son after son to Jacob, each one like a stab delivered to her own heart, while she tried so desperately to conceive and failed. Each child born to her sister was a reminder of her failure, and a death blow to her hopes of motherhood. She began to think that she would never conceive, and the thought threatened to sink her into a whirlpool of utter despair.

What use am I to anyone, she thought; barren, and forced to share my husband's love with another.

Everything else having let her down, she found herself praying in desperation to Jacob's God.

"Oh, please," she implored, sinking to her knees before a deity that she was not even certain she believed in, "I beg You, give me a son that my reproach of barrenness will be removed."

And she wept and cried out with all the frustrated anguish that possessed her soul.

They all moved about as if dazed. This was a special day, a day they all thought would never come, yet it had finally arrived. Even Leah found herself rejoicing on Jacob's behalf.

Rachel had conceived and just been delivered of a healthy boy. She named him Joseph, "he who adds" because even as she brought Joseph into the world she asked that the Lord would give her yet another son to add to his number.

From the very first there was something special about this child that set him apart from his older brothers. He opened his eyes and looked directly into the eyes of both parents with all of the calm intelligence of a much older child, and did not fuss when hungry but simply tugged at the neckline of his mother's robe when he wanted to nurse. It was soon evident that his father was enamored of him from the moment he held him in his arms, a fact that would eventually come to dismay his other sons, and the mother who had borne them.

For Joseph would have a place in heart of his father that none other could ever fill or supplant, although there would be those who would vainly attempt it.

Chapter 11
The Plan

It was now twenty years since Jacob had invaded the lives of Leah and Rachel. The years had brought many changes, the least of which was the large family that the two marriages with its rivalry between the sisters had produced. Eleven sons and one daughter now sat around the family table, and they kept their mothers busily employed with the care of them. Jacob's oldest son Reuben was now twelve years old and his youngest son Joseph but an infant.

Jacob suddenly thought with longing of his homeland in Canaan and the promise that awaited him there, of the mantle of the patriarchs that he would one day assume from his father Isaac. He fretted as he wondered how his parents fared, and what had become of his brother, Esau. He had toiled hard for his father-in-law Laban, but it was time for him to move on with his family and establish a home that they could call their own.

He decided it was time to ask for his freedom.

"Laban," he said one day to the older man, "I wish to take my wives and the children and go. It is time that we had a home of our own, and we have grown so numerous that it is costly for you to support us."

Although he was surprised at this unexpected statement from his son-in-law, this seemed fair to Laban. A man should have a home of his own, at least a man who was worthy of the name, and it was true that his house was becoming crowded with all of Jacob's boys. Not that he didn't enjoy his grandchildren, but his own growing sons added to the mix made the combination overwhelming at times as the house rang with the sound of laughter, quarrels, and roughhousing as fourteen boys exercised their dominion of the family quarters.

"What shall I give you as your parting wages?" Laban asked Jacob.

"Why, nothing at all," Jacob answered. "Just do one thing for me and I will pasture your flock for you: allow me to pass through the flock today and remove every speckled and spotted sheep and every black lamb, along with the spotted and speckled goats. And they shall be my wages.

"If you find any goats with me that are not speckled or spotted, or any white lambs, then you can consider them stolen."

Laban agreed and they arranged for Jacob to take his choice.

The next night Jacob was roused from a fitful slumber and tossed about trying to recapture his sleep. A sound had waked him; but he could not tell what it was, or even where it came from. He decided at last to walk about and see whether the night air might make him sleepy.

As he entered the porch he heard a noise and quickly drew back into the shadows in the corner of it. Overhead he heard the sound of voices, and what they said startled him and brought him fully awake.

"It is not fair," said Beor. "Our father has given Jacob the best of our flock and so robbed us of our inheritance. Shall we tolerate it?"

"No, we shall not," stated Alub. "Those goats and lambs belong to *us*; who is this Jacob that he should take what belongs to our father and therefore to us?"

"Then we must make this clear to our father," said Beor. "Let him know that we will not tolerate this man Jacob who has come here and caused nothing but trouble for our family."

"That is right," said Alub. "Why, just look at the misery he has caused our sisters. Neither of them is happy; and can you blame them?"

Jacob did not stay to hear anymore.

The next day he observed Laban and noticed the dramatic change in his attitude. He was not his usual friendly self; he did not greet Jacob with his customary broad smile that threatened to run off of his face but instead frowned when Jacob entered the room where the family had assembled to break their fast. Indeed, Laban broke off what he was saying and was unusually silent throughout the meal. He said nothing more, but bestowed frowns upon his daughters and grandsons as well as Jacob.

And Jacob felt an ominous foreboding rise from deep within his soul.

Later that day he sent for Leah and Rachel to come to him secretly in the field where he was working.

"We must prepare to leave for Canaan but

we must do so in absolute secrecy. Your father's heart has inexplicably changed toward me, and I do not like it. I waited on the Lord this morning when I came to the field, and He told me to return to the land of my fathers and He would be with me and bless me in this undertaking.

"You know that I have served Laban faithfully, but he continually has tried to cheat me, not once but several times over the years."

Here Leah flinched and Rachel cleared her throat; Jacob swallowed hard and hastened to continue.

"He has changed my wages ten times over the years, never fulfilling what he has promised. Yet God has been faithful and has not allowed the changes to hurt me. If Laban promised me specked goats for my wages then the whole flock brought forth speckled. If he said I should have the striped then they all birthed striped.

"But I can no longer count on him to keep his word to me, or even to you, his daughters. We must gather the children and the maids, along with those of our own household after nightfall and take all that we possess; for we shall never return here. Let us meet after the household has fallen asleep and leave as quietly as possible so that we may be well gone by daybreak, and before our flight is discovered."

It was not an easy task to prepare the children. They lay sleeping in the house not far from the rooms of Laban's sons, and none of them had ever been known to be quiet, even at the times when they fell sick. At those times their mothers and brothers must entertain them and keep their attention occupied, as none of them liked to keep still and sleep was something they did not like to do in the middle of the day when there was so much going on that they feared to miss anything.

Rachel bit her lip as Dan and Naphtali dawdled and yawned loudly, not understanding the need to rise in the middle of the night or the necessity to be quiet while doing so. Little Joseph she merely scooped up in her arms and he nestled close and was quiet; but her sons through her maid Bilhah were stubborn and contrary, attempting to make her laugh with their antics, making funny faces at her and giggling at one another's hilarious efforts.

It was Leah who solved the dilemma. She looked at Reuben, who simply hoisted the two youngsters over his shoulders and bounced them up and down, telling them that unless they shut up at once and did as they were told he would drop them on their heads.

They had one moment of panic when Issachar, irate at being waked out of a sound sleep, pulled the hair of his sister Dinah as an outlet for his frustrations. The little girl shrieked, but Leah promptly clapped a hand over her mouth. When the startled child's eyes filled with tears and she inhaled deeply to release a mighty sob, Leah turned it into a game and clapped her hand lightly over her mouth again, then released it and clapped it over it again until her daughter erupted into a gale of giggles.

"Shhh!" Leah cautioned and dropped a

kiss on the top of Dinah's head of rich brown curls.

At last all were assembled in the field farthest from the house, where Jacob had taken the precaution to hide the goats and lambs of his own flocks earlier in the day, just before the household assembled for the evening meal. Had he done it any earlier he would have risked discovery by Laban, but once everyone came in for the last meal of the day none ventured out into the fields again.

He put his anxious wives and bewildered children on camels and tied his flocks together with long cords of heavy rope so that none of them would be lost. Reuben had finally persuaded the younger children to be quiet, and one look at their father's face confirmed that he would brook no antics or rebellion. He gave them the intense stare under straightened eyebrows that they knew so well and immediately stilled their active bodies and hushed their voices. The boys exchanged puzzled glances with each other but made haste to obey the command of their older brother after seeing it reflected in their father's eyes.

Leah cast one sorrowful glance backward at the house where she had grown up and been married, knowing in her heart that she would never see it again. She grieved not for the house but for her gentle mother, who had always been her comfort and abiding strength. She could not help but weep a little, but turned her face away so that the others did not see. Her place was with her husband, wherever he went, and she knew it. Yet how she would miss the counsel and wisdom of the woman who had guided her through the sea of confusion that her life frequently resembled!

Rachel did not glance back at the house, nor did she grieve at all. Although she would genuinely miss her mother, she would be glad to never see again the father who had ruined her life by tricking her betrothed into marrying her sister and forcing the two of them to share him. No; she would not miss her father, but she had left something for Laban to remember her by.

She had stolen his teraphim and hidden them in her baggage, lest he attempt to call on them and use their power to track the fugitives.

Chapter 12
The Curse

It was a difficult journey over rugged terrain and dusty primitive roads that were barely a track in the wilderness, hampered by the tired children who grew crosser with every passing mile, fretting for food and longing to get down from the camels and stretch their weary legs.

Little Joseph fared the easiest. He was carried in his mother's arms and when he was hungry she was able to nurse him under the cover of her mantle. The others were not so fortunate, and as night turned into day started demanding that they be fed, and at once.

Here Jacob decided that a break was necessary. There had been no time to assemble much to eat, and he had settled for taking a few loaves of bread from the kitchen after the household had gone to bed. He did not dare assemble anything before the retirement of the household, lest the servants notice that food was missing and report it to their master.

Jacob jumped down from his camel and handed the reins to Leah, who caught them quickly and secured them to her saddle. Then he took a loaf from his saddle bag and broke off several pieces which he distributed to the hungry children. Leah had had the forethought to secure a couple of jars of honey from the storage room and deftly smeared a generous quantity on the slices of bread, which brought exclamations of delight from the hungry little brood.

Tears dried quickly and turned to happy smiles as Jacob tousled each little head and gave them water from the large skin he had filled before they left the house of Laban. After each child had been fed and watered he took the reins of his camel back from Leah and bade the animal to bow so that he could mount back up.

They were soon on their way again but the weary children now cried for sleep. Jacob rued that they had been deprived of it, as it had been necessary to leave while Laban and his family slept so that they could leave cloaked in secrecy in the shadows of night, as well as to get a generous start ahead of them before it was discovered that they were missing from the household.

With a sigh and a glance at the rapidly rising sun, he searched about him for a place where he might hide his family and his flocks before his father-in-law caught up with them. Seeing nothing but a grove of olive trees, he once again dismounted and gathered up the children and placed them under the shade of the thickest trees. In truth, he was as weary as they, but he tethered his flocks and camels together and mounted watch while his wives and children slept for a few precious hours, all the while knowing that each minute brought the pursuit of his enraged father-in-law nearer to them.

It was, in fact, quite some time before Laban caught up with them. He had been taken ill the very night that Jacob and his family fled, and no one had dared to tell him of their flight, for fear that he might die of shock when the news was imparted that his daughters and grandchildren were gone without any warning or farewell. When he was told on the third day, he was furious that the news had been withheld from him, and gathered about him all of the men he knew to help him in his search.

"Quickly!" he said to his sons, "gather all of the men we know in Haran. Tell them I have desperate need of their help. Summon them to come at once and we shall depart immediately."

Laban ensured that he would have additional help in tracking his daughters and grandchildren. He made at once for the cupboard where he kept his idols, so that he might call on them at need. Never had he felt such urgency for their assistance as he did on this day.

He whipped open the door of the cupboard, only to discover that the shelves were empty.

Ten days after their flight, Jacob and his wives and children were camping in the hill country of Gilead. The hills were beautiful and rose to great heights, casting shadows against one another so that the one behind another looked like a desert mirage. The effect was ethereal and unearthly, and made one stop to gasp in admiration. The hills were heavily forested and the trees provided welcome shade for the weary travelers, who eagerly spurred their camels on for one last burst of strength before scrambling down from them to cast themselves on the ground, where they lay on their backs and stretched their arms overhead, and exhaled sighs of relief from the exhausting days of strenuous travel.

The children found it delightful and spent much time chasing one another and hiding behind the many trees, shrieking with laughter whenever one was caught by another. Despite his anxiety, the sight brought a smile to the lips of Jacob, and he was pleased that they could find something to laugh about in spite of having fled the only home they ever knew and leaving their beloved grandmother, who no doubt was grieving their loss along with that of her daughters.

They decided to camp here until Jacob could plan the next step. He was uncertain where to go, having been told only to go the land of his ancestors. And he was haunted by the thought of an encounter with his brother.

Did Esau still bear a grudge; and if so, did he still desire his death?

They heard their advent before they saw them. The sound of braying camels and the thunder of their hooves betrayed the presence of their pursuers. At last they had been tracked and their hiding place discovered.

Jacob glanced with trepidation at his wives, who quickly gathered the children and hustled them into the tents. It was too late to even attempt to leave, but they wished to put the children out of harm's way, should any violence erupt. In truth, Jacob did not know what to expect. He had never had fair dealings with Laban and did not expect that to change now that he had left without a farewell, taking his wives and children with him.

He went out alone to meet him.

Laban glowered at Jacob.

"Why have you done this to me?" he growled. "You stole my daughters away as if they were your captives, and gave me no opportunity to send them off with a proper farewell! I would have given them a feast and had song and dance on their behalf, with games for the little ones, but you took them away and my grandchildren with them before I could give them a parting kiss and a warm embrace."

Here Laban shook his head and a sob escaped his throat. Jacob felt a momentary compunction at depriving his father-in-law of the family he loved, yet knew in his heart that he could not trust this man. Laban's next words confirmed the accuracy of this perception.

"I could do you great harm if I wish to do so," Laban snarled. "I have brought many men with me, as you can see, and they stand ready to do my bidding. Whatever I ask, they have sworn with an oath to carry out."

He pointed to the assembly who stood off in the distance, waiting for a signal from Laban.

Laban's next words, however, startled Jacob greatly, and awed his soul with a sense of wonder.

"But as I slept last night your God appeared to me in a dream," Laban continued, his statement surprising Jacob. "And He warned me to not speak any ill of you, so I will restrain my curses. I have seen that He is mighty, and I do not wish to incur His wrath against me.

"But I have this against *you*: why did you steal my teraphim? They are of no use to you, and I have need of them. Where are they?

"Answer me and surrender them to me at once!"

And Laban bellowed this last command with the anger of a wounded beast. His face turned red with his fury, and he glared at his son-in-law with eyes that glittered like black agates in his crimson countenance.

Jacob made haste to appease him for the sake of his wives and children; not for the world would he wish any harm to come to them, and for their sake humbled himself before the man who had cheated him so often.

"I was afraid that you would take your daughters from me by force if you knew I was leaving; and that is something that I could not bear. But I swear that I know nothing of the theft of your gods.

"I give you permission to search our tents and to take anything you find that belongs to you, but do not expect to find the idols here, as none of us have any need of them. And if by some chance someone *did* take them, for reasons that I cannot fathom, then know that that person shall not live."

Laban scrambled into Jacob's tent and made a thorough search of the interior. He looked in his bedding, behind every pole, and even in the flaps. But his search yielded nothing for which he sought.

He hastened to Leah's tent, where she and the boys greeted him with cries of joy that detained him for a moment as he exchanged an embrace with his daughter and kissed his grandsons and little Dinah. But even this happy reunion did not distract him long from his mission.

Next he searched the tents of the handmaids Bilhah and Zilpah. They were astonished to see him and permitted him with modestly downcast eyes to look through their humble belongings. But the teraphim were not there.

Finally he came to Rachel's tent. She had hidden the teraphim in her camel's saddle bag and was sitting upon it. When her father greeted her she calmly gave him a detached smile and apologized for not rising, but she was indisposed in the customary manner of women and could not do so.

Her father gave her a strained smile, embarrassed at the implication and hastened out of her tent lest something unpleasant meet his gaze.

He turned at last to Jacob with mounting frustration.

"I *know* they are here, Jacob. They were in my home before you left, and now they are missing. One of you stole them, and I know it, although I cannot prove it."

Jacob shrugged his shoulders, exasperated at the other man's insistence. He had done all that was asked of him and there was nothing further he could do to placate him.

"I am sorry, Laban, but you did search and your search yielded nothing. I am certain that no one in my household would have need of your gods.

"And as I said before, if anyone *did* take them, then that person will pay with their life."

Chapter 13
The Covenant

Jacob had borne with the discovery by his pursuer and the insult of the search as patiently as he was able. But now he could contain himself no longer and vented his exasperation to the fullest.

"What harm have I ever done you, that you should pursue me with such an assembly of armed men?" he exploded at Laban. "I gave you leave to search through all my possessions for anything that was stolen from you, yet you found nothing belonging to you. How could you possibly accuse me of theft?

"Have you found anything belonging to you? If so, set it here where all may see it, and then you can judge me to be a thief.

"I have served you faithfully for twenty years, and all that time you received the blessing of the Lord solely because I was with you!

"Did any of your ewes or female goats have a miscarriage? No! And I never touched a ram of your flock to eat it. If any of the flock was torn apart by wild beasts I took the loss from my own flock and recompensed you by giving you one of my own. Indeed, you would have required no less of me, although I was innocent of any wrong!

"I served you with hard labor in the heat of the day when I could barely stand before the blazing sun, and in the cold of night when I longed to lay down my weary head, and went without sleep when it was required of me. I served you for fourteen years for your daughters, and six years I served to acquire a flock of my own in repayment for my service. During that time you changed my wages six times, so that I never knew what I could count on. You have served me ill, Laban.

"Had it not been for the God of my fathers and the vengeance you would have reaped from my father, no doubt you would have sent me away with nothing at all, and taken my wives, my children, and all the flocks that you promised me and left me with nothing to call my own.

"But God has seen my affliction and your ill treatment of me, and so He warned you last night to bring no harm to me."

Laban listened to this unexpected outburst from his usually obedient son-in-law with growing fury. Clearly Jacob's fear of mistreatment at the hands of this man was justified to those who witnessed this scene. Laban glared at Jacob with an unrelenting stare that did not flinch as he answered his son-in-law's tirade of vented frustration, accumulated from many years of bitterness at the injustice meted out to him by the older man.

"All that you have belongs to *me*!" Laban flared. "Your wives are *my* daughters, your sons are *my* grandchildren, and every goat and lamb in your possession I gave to you. The law would not find me guilty if I took everything away from you and left you destitute, for it was mine to give you at my pleasure in the first place!"

A gasp from Leah, who came to stand in the doorway of her tent that she might observe her husband and father, broke through Laban's fury. He sighed deeply and glanced back at her and young Reuben who had joined her in the doorway with a deep sadness in his dark eyes.

"Nevertheless," he began, "I can not bring myself to hurt them. And it would wound them grievously to be parted from their husband and father."

A small sob escaped Leah's lips and Laban smiled at her ruefully before turning back with a heavy sigh to Jacob.

"For their sake, let us make a covenant between us," Laban said, "and it will be a witness between the two of us. If you are willing, that is."

Jacob gave his father-in-law a wary glance. How long would Laban keep his word? If he kept it at all.

But he realized that he had no choice but to go along with the older man's suggestion.

Jacob found a large stone and set it in place as a pillar. He and his sons gathered more stones and heaped them into a pile. When he had finished he turned to Laban.

"I shall call it Jegar-sahadutha," Laban pronounced in his tongue of Aramaic.

Jacob, however, had a different name for it.

"It shall be called Galeed," he said in the Hebrew dialect.

In both tongues the meaning was the same; a witness or watchtower.

"This heap is a witness between you and me," Laban answered his son-in-law. "May the

Lord watch between you and me when we are absent from one another."

Jacob nodded his head in agreement and searched his father-in-law's face for any signs of duplicity, but he could detect none.

Laban in turn stared at him, and then nodded his head as if satisfied and continued.

"If you mistreat my daughters, or take other wives in addition to them, God will see it and be a witness between us.

"Behold the heap and the pillar I have set between us; they are a witness. I shall not pass by this heap and pillar to you to do harm, and you shall not pass by this heap and pillar to me to do harm. Let it be known that the God of Abraham and the God of Nahor, Who was the God of their father, shall judge betwcen us."

Jacob bowed his head and closed his eyes, overcome by the mention of his kinsmen. He opened his eyes and nodded his head in agreement at Laban. Then he lifted his right hand to heaven.

"I swear by the God of my fathers."

Jacob slaughtered a goat and offered it as a sacrifice to the Lord to seal the covenant. When it had been solemnly offered he and his family made a meal of it, bidding Laban to join them.

It was a bittersweet moment, for in their hearts they knew it unlikely that they would ever see the older man again. The journey to Canaan would be a long one, and not one that was convenient to repeat often. And scoundrel though he could be, still, Laban was the father of Jacob's wives and the grandfather of his children, and therefore a beloved member of his family.

They spent the evening after the meal was consumed with singing songs of their peoples and telling the tales that had been passed down from one generation to the next for so many years that they had lost the count of them.

And in the morning Laban arose and took a sorrowful leave of his daughters and grandchildren, and gave them each a tender kiss of farewell, and departed for his own land.

Chapter 14
Jacob Meets A Man

After Laban had taken his leave of them the family was subdued, each one lost in their memories of the old man.

Leah remembered the time she had overheard him speaking to her mother about how difficult it would be to find a husband for a disfigured daughter.

"Just look at her!" he bellowed. "What good will she bring me? No man wants damaged goods, and her eyes make her look like she spent the night crying, and may start doing so again. Does any man want a weeping wife? No! She should be cheerful and always encouraging.

"The girl doesn't stand a chance, I tell you."

Even today Leah remembered the fierce stab that had pierced her heart at hearing those sharp words. If a knife had penetrated her robe and the blade stabbed her it would not have been any more painful than the fiery agony that she felt at her father's wounding but accurate summation of her dismal marriage chances.

What hurt even more was her mother agreeing with him.

"Now, now, Laban," she lulled in her soothing voice, "it is not the girl's fault. Leah is a sweet girl; it may be that some man may yet want her."

"Truly?" her husband asked in a voice dripping with sarcasm.

Leah heard Adinah hesitate before

responding.

"Well, probably not," she admitted, with the sound of rueful regret that more than anything betrayed her reluctant agreement with her husband's assessment of their daughter's lack of marital chances.

"But one never knows. There is always the possibility of a widower with small children left to him to raise alone. Not every woman will take on another woman's brood, and Leah is wonderful with children and they love her. It may yet be that some man may look beyond her appearance and see the mother's heart that she possesses."

Leah did not linger to hear any more of her parents' dire predictions for her loveless future. She put a hand over her mouth to stifle the sobs of hurt that threatened to escape her lips, and crept quietly away with all the stealth she could muster, and went to her bedchamber and lay looking up at the ceiling, too wounded even for tears.

Rachel thought bitterly of the man she blamed for ruining her life and the assurance of success that had been so happily planned for her. Even to this day she was devastated at the way he had tricked Jacob into marrying Leah as well as herself. Had she had Jacob to herself instead of being forced to share him with another (let alone her own sister!) they would no doubt had been happier than they were.

How galling that she had to watch as her sister bore son after son to the man to whom she had betrothed herself and waited seven long years for the promise to be fulfilled. Why, most girls were already married at the age when she had promised herself to Jacob! Had she not proved her love by waiting patiently and refusing any other offers for her hand?

And how many there had been! Why, she was the most sought after maiden in all of Haran! But she had refused all offers in order to marry her cousin Jacob, who had captivated her the moment they met when he had kissed her in the custom of greeting, and she found herself suddenly wishing that there had been more to that kiss than the greeting between cousins.

Sometimes she felt her love had turned to hatred when she saw him smiling softly at Leah, or making arrangements to visit her bed while temporarily forsaking Rachel's. Surely he must have *some* feelings for Leah to act in such a manner! Otherwise he would have left off visiting her after she had borne him a few sons, let alone six of them.

And although her pride refused to admit it even to herself, she was occasionally plagued by the thought that Jacob could very well have refused to visit Leah at all once her bridal week was dutifully completed and he was at last married to the bride of his dreams for which he had labored so long. Yet, he did *not* forsake Leah, and she bore him one son after the other, while Rachel wondered why this man who loved her still sought her sister's bed...

Her thoughts turned to the stolen teraphim, and a cold shiver swept through her body. Jacob had said whoever had stolen the idols would die; but he did not know that she had taken them. Therefore, she was safe from all harm, as he would never put a member of his family to death.

She was confident in that after witnessing his lenient dealings with her own father who had cheated him time and again. Yet he had given him a farewell feast and sent him off with the kisses and embraces of his wives and children, who would sorely miss the old man. If he could be lenient with Laban, surely he would never harm a hair on Rachel's head!

Yet, why did this sense of foreboding flood her soul?

Jacob mused on the years he had served Laban for his wives and flocks, and how often the wily old jackal had tricked him out of his wages, even substituting one daughter for another. He sometimes wondered what would have happened if Leah had been more attractive and some other man had wanted her before he came along. Would Laban have allowed him to serve only seven years for Rachel, and then given her to him as his bride?

Or had Laban merely used his daughters as an excuse, and his true aim was free labor from Jacob in exchange for a roof over his head and taking his daughters off of his hands?

In the cool of the evening the family sat around talking after they had partaken of their final meal of the day. Now that Laban had come and gone and would no longer be a part of their lives there was a sense of ease and calm. The terrible anxiety that had stemmed from fear of his pursuit was alleviated and all could relax. Grief at his farewell had turned to reminiscing of the past, but only the grandchildren had fond memories of the grandfather who had genuinely loved them and been proud of them, delighting in everything they said and did.

Reuben recalled the day that Laban had told him the story of his people, and that he must remember that he came from a remarkable family, on both his father's and his mother's side.

"And you will carry on our traditions and bear the mantle of leadership, my boy," Laban had said with tears in his eyes as the child grew tall and straight with strong limbs and ruddy health.

Naphtali had his memories as well.

"I will miss Grandfather tossing me in the air and catching me again," he said as he woefully shook his head at the thought that such a delight was to be no more.

Rachel smoothed his curls and he wrapped his little arms around her neck and hid his face in her mane of dark hair to hide the tears that he considered unmanly and did not wish his brothers to see.

Simeon and Judah sighed as they too remembered the tossing and catching by the old man when they were younger and what fun it had been.

"Well, I suppose we were getting too big to be tossed anyway," Simeon said somewhat philosophically.

It was silent for some time, as each was lost in thought. The moon had risen and the first stars made their appearance, twinkling their silvery lights in the expanse above. The sound of a jackal in the distance startled little Joseph, who began to cry in alarm.

Leah proposed putting the children to bed and everyone retiring for the night. Rachel agreed that this was a good idea, and they gathered up the boys, who protested that they were not tired. Their remonstrances were met with firm instructions by the sisters to obey their bidding and one by one they were trundled off to bed in their tents.

Jacob alone remained up. He felt that the day was not yet over for him, but could not say why he felt that way. Something made him alert and watchful, and his eyes scanned the horizon for any sign of trouble that would give him a clue to his wariness.

There was nothing.

Still, he could not shake his feeling of restlessness and decided to take a walk. Perhaps the cool crisp air of the evening would clear his brain and refresh his body.

Jacob wandered about roaming the land. It was rugged and mountainous, with slanting slopes full of loose stone that could trip the unwary and send a donkey hurtling headlong. He carried a staff for better navigation, placing it before him to anchor in the ground.

When he had traveled some distance, he was startled to see a group of armed men approaching. They were taller than the men of his people, and clothed in pure white linen that looked like the snow on the mountaintops. He was suddenly struck with a strange sense of awe mixed with fear.

His heart started beating rapidly and his mouth went dry; there was something unusual about these men...He came to a halt and wondered if he should retrace his steps and avoid meeting them. After debating briefly his curiosity overcame his fear, so he stopped and waited for them to reach him.

As they neared they put up their hands in the symbol for peace. Jacob saluted them in return. His heart began pounding faster in his chest, for no discernible reason that he could see. There was something very strange about these men...

"We come in peace from the Most High," the tallest of them proclaimed.

The announcement stunned Jacob. Surely they could not be...

Another man nodded and spoke in turn.

"You are entering the territory of your brother Esau."

Abruptly the entire company turned on their heel and walked back in the direction from which they had come. Jacob watched their departure until they disappeared from his sight. When they had left him he marveled and stood silent.

In awe he breathed out, "Surely they were the Lord's army!"

And he named the place where they had appeared Manahaim.

The next morning he hastily summoned

his servants.

He evaluated them silently, pondering on what he knew of each of them.

That one is timid, so he will not do, he thought of one young boy who was barely into his teens. That one is too old and cannot keep pace with the others, he mused as he considered another. That one has a good head on his shoulders and will give wise counsel to the others, he thought of a third. That one is a swift runner and can run ahead of the others as a scout, he deemed a fourth.

At last when he had considered them all he chose messengers from among them. They stood silently and awaited his orders.

"I am sending you to the land of Edom, to my brother Esau. Tell him that I have spent many years with my father-in-law Laban; and that I am sending him a gift of the finest of my flocks and my donkeys.

"And tell him that I honor him as my lord in the land where he rules."

Jacob spent many anxious hours until his messengers returned. He wondered about his brother; had Esau changed very much? Was he still fiery of temperament and foolish in his decisions? Or had life taught him the lessons he had refused to learn from their parents?

Only seeing him will tell me, Jacob thought.

He wondered in his heart whether he was eager or fearful to see his twin. True, they had never been close, always having been so different. But they were of the same blood and had played together tolerably well as children. It was only when they grew older that their differences had begun to show, and their ambitions and desires divided them; Jacob, the peace-loving one who preferred a quiet life and cared for their people, and Esau, the hunter who enjoyed the delights of the flesh and cared only for his appetites.

He still feared the wrath of his brother, and wondered whether Esau still desired his death. Yet he longed for a sight of his family, to see one of his own people. Too long had he been a stranger in Haran. Although he had acquired a family of his own with wives and children, he realized he missed his homeland and his own kin...

And so it was with mixed emotions that Jacob awaited the return of his messengers.

When they returned to Jacob the following day the news they brought back with them was ominous.

"Your brother Esau is heading this way to meet you with four hundred men."

The news made Jacob's heart stop beating. He looked around him at his wives and children, and all of their servants. He felt that his question regarding his brother's sentiment toward him was answered. Surely Esau would not hesitate to kill them all in revenge for what his brother had done to him. Indeed, he might very well take a vengeful delight in destroying all that Jacob loved the most.

He paused to consider what to do and quickly devised a plan.

"Take with you the finest of my flocks and donkeys. They shall be a peace offering to my brother Esau," he instructed the servants, who made haste to do his bidding, quickly dispersing to judge the animals and take only the finest with them.

He then turned to his wives, who stood gazing intently at him awaiting his direction.

"Leah, you take half of the children and the servants with you and head west. Rachel, you take the other half with you and head east. Then if Esau attacks one half, the other half will surely escape."

Then Jacob let out a moan and looked upward and raised his palms to the sky.

"Oh, God of my fathers, I am Your servant. You said that if I returned to the land of my fathers that you would prosper me. I am not worthy of the love and mercy You have shown me. See how You have blessed me; I crossed the river Jordan twenty years ago with nothing but a staff and now I have two companies of people with wives and children. I pray that you protect them and protect me from the wrath of my brother Esau; for you promised to make a great nation of me, with descendants too numerous to be counted. Deliver us from his hand, I pray, that the promise You made might be fulfilled."

He sent them ahead, the children protesting at yet another journey, but he was firm.

"Do as I tell you!" he said. "I will see you shortly."

He earnestly hoped that last statement

was true.

He saw them off, sending them across the ford of Jabbok, his heart pounding as he watched them go. With agony he witnessed the departure of Rachel and little Joseph as they headed away from him, and the sight of Leah and the little troop that followed after her tore at his heart. He watched until they were all out of sight. Then he wandered among the banks and hid in the reeds waiting for the approach of Esau and his men.

He scarcely breathed in his concern for his family and prayed they would reach safety. His rapidly beating heart pulsed in his throat, and beads of sweat dripped from his brow onto his nose. He made no move to wipe his face, fearful of making any noise that would betray his presence. He licked the sweat from his upper lip and restrained himself from scratching as the reeds poked into his robe, irritating his skin.

It seemed an eternity since he had watched his wives depart with his children, and he grew weary in his watch. His body ached and his legs began to cramp, stuck in the same position for so long. Occasionally a gnat flew up into his face and buzzed past his ear. He resisted the temptation to swat it away, knowing that he must remain quiet in order to escape detection for as long as possible.

His precautions proved in vain, however, for suddenly he was struck and knocked to the ground, winding him. For a moment he lay stunned and was unable to breathe, the air escaping his lungs with a gasp and a sharp pain tore through his chest; but a second blow roused anger within him. How dare Esau come to him and attack him from behind, like a thief or a vagabond! Such was not the behavior of an honorable man!

He pushed himself up with all of his strength only to be knocked back down again. He attempted to rise again but before he could raise himself to his knees he was struck and knocked down again. Anger rose within him and a fierce determination to strike back rose within him. But he could not lift himself due to the rain of blows that descended on him from behind.

At last he turned onto his back and stared into the face of his assailant.

It was not Esau.

He did not know who it was but the man was determined to best him. Jacob thrust upward in a vain attempt to push the man off of him, but it was of no use. The man simply pushed down and thrust all of his weight upon him.

"Who are you?" Jacob demanded. "What have I ever done to you that you attack me in this manner?"

The man did not reply but merely continued to push down on Jacob, who now remembered a trick that he and Esau used to use when they were boys and wrestled in play. He thrust his leg up between the man's thighs and pushed upward. The move caught the man off guard and he went flying over Jacob's head. Jacob now pounced on the man where he lay on the ground but the other man was not finished yet.

He quickly flipped Jacob over on his back and started pummeling him. Jacob had the wind knocked out of him once again but this time he punched back at his foe. To his frustration, however, the man seemed tireless, and nothing deterred him in his senseless and unprovoked attack. If Jacob punched him the man hit back. If the man flipped Jacob over, Jacob twisted beneath him and kicked at his attacker.

They continued in this manner throughout the night. The moon had risen and the stars twinkled overhead. The hooting of an owl came from a tree nearby. The sound of rippling water was heard as an animal splashed into the river, and the breaking of twigs came from the shore as another animal ran on the banks.

The darkness began to fade as the first rays of light made their appearance, and the stars faded in the sky. Overhead, the moon still shone but with less luster now that the ebon of night gave way to the gray shadows of dawn.

Jacob would not have believed that a struggle of this sort could have lasted so long, but he was determined not to give in and the other man refused to stop his attack. Over and over they punched and wrestled and flipped each other overhead, each with an unwavering determination to prevail, but each unable to best his opponent. Jacob now found breathing difficult but he could not take time to pause and catch his breath, as his assailant never let up for even a moment.

Jacob heard the reeds begin to rustle as a breeze swept through the riverbed. The gentle puff of air cooled his hot cheeks and he realized suddenly that he was thirsty and wished that he could take a refreshing drink from the river to wet his dry throat. Such wishing was fruitless, however, as the man who fought with him only seemed to intensify his attack all the more, and Jacob began to feel that he and the man had always been locked in this struggle, through long months and weary years, always striving with none prevailing...

Finally, as the sun rose overhead with rosy fingers creeping across the gray remnants of the night that sent the wisps of shadows fleeing, the man put his finger on Jacob's thigh.

A searing pain shot through him as the thigh was dislocated. Jacob groaned in agony and felt as though his skin had been set on fire. It was this mere touch and the injury that followed that gave Jacob an inkling of who this Man might be...

"Let me go, for the day is breaking," the Man said to Jacob.

Jacob was now certain.

"No, I shall not let go unless you bless me," he said.

"What is your name?" the Man asked.

"It is Jacob," he responded.

And he thought of what the name meant; cheater, supplanter, thief. And had he not done as much to his brother Esau? Had he not cheated him twice and brought suffering on the twin who had never sought to harm him?

He was torn from his somber reverie by the next words of the Man.

"It is no longer Jacob, but Israel," the Man

answered, "for you have strived with God and man and have prevailed."

Jacob looked up at the Man, scarcely breathing. The sun blinded him and he could not see the Man's face clearly. Indeed, it was partly hidden by the hood of the cloak he wore that Jacob did not notice until now.

"Please, tell me your name," he implored.

"Why do you ask?" the Man replied. "But I *do* bless you. I bless the fruit of your loins, the crops of your fields, and promise that in all you do you shall prosper."

Jacob rose slowly and with great pain from the bed of reeds and limped to his feet, catching his breath as he did so. It was a limp he would have for the rest of his life. It would bring him both pride at prevailing with God, and humility at having the audacity to have attempted to do so.

Jacob named the place where he had wrestled with the Man Penuel. And he marveled.

"I have seen God face to face, but my life is preserved."

Chapter 15
The Brothers

Jacob crossed the ford and soon found his family much more quickly than he had expected, not far away from the banks. They had made uneasy camp there for the night, setting a guard to watch for the advent of Esau and his men, and were just rousing with the breaking of day. He urged them to rise quickly and make ready to flee for Esau would probably be nearing them soon and there was not a moment to be lost.

But it was already too late.

The sound of hooves thundered on the horizon, and lifting his hand to his eyes to shield them from the blinding rays of the rising sun, Jacob spied a cloud of dust that grew rapidly until it seemed to fill the vista before him. Without warning his heart stopped beating and lost his breath. He swayed unsteadily on his feet, suddenly weary with his sleepless night and the relentless attack he had endured. For a moment he could not breathe, try though he might to gulp air into his lungs, then he remembered his wives and children and the need to take prompt action for their safety.

"Quickly," he breathed as he addressed the maids, "Bilhah, you take Dan and Naphtali. Zilpah, take Gad and Asher.

"Leah, you follow behind them with Reuben, Simeon, Levi, Judah, Issachar, Zebulun, and Dinah. Children, listen to your mothers!"

They turned frightened and bewildered eyes upon them, and the eyes of Dinah filled with tears. But there was no time to reassure them or to comfort his daughter. They must flee for their lives.

Last of all he turned to Rachel. He looked deeply into her eyes and spoke through them all that he longed to say. She saw it and flushed, and a sparkle rose to her own eyes despite the danger they faced.

"And Rachel, you and Joseph must go last."

He went ahead of them and walked to meet the approaching company of four hundred men, all of whom he expected would be fully armed and equipped with spears and knives. The ground shook beneath their camels as they ran swiftly to meet Jacob and his family. Jacob leaned on his staff, his thigh bothering him and the lack of sleep beginning to make itself felt. He mentally shook his head and strived to keep focused on the emergency of the moment, knowing that he could not afford to make a mistake in this encounter that he had dreaded for twenty years with the brother who hated him so violently.

At last he saw a man that rode ahead of the rest of the company. Jacob walked to meet him and bowed low to the ground. He bowed again. And again; seven times in all. The man laughed and alit from his camel.

It was Esau.

Jacob looked up into the face of his brother with trepidation at his present danger and with curiosity to see what changes the years had brought. The years had but added to his strength, and he looked like a lion of a man. He was still heavily muscled, and there was the hot light of the predator in the depths of his brown eyes. His tawny mane of wavy locks and hairy arms gave him the appearance of a wild cat that prowled in search of prey.

Jacob only hoped that the prey would not be his family.

Esau sat motionless as he looked down on the sight of his younger brother prostrating himself at his feet. A dry chuckle escaped his lips; a chuckle that nevertheless held in its tone all the bitterness of their last meeting. Then his face contorted without warning and the chuckle turned abruptly to a sob that was quickly cut off.

"Jacob!" Esau cried as he jumped from his camel, not even waiting for the animal to lower itself so that he might gradually descend from its heights.

He bounded over to his Jacob and raised him to his feet and embraced him fervently. He gave him the kiss of peace and wept as the tears racked his body, burying his face in his brother's neck.

Jacob was astonished at the wave of emotion that swept through him suddenly, and tears erupted before he knew they were coming. The brothers stood in an embrace for several moments, weeping and muttering words that only they could hear. But to the relief of all those that surrounded them it was evident that the meeting would not end in bloodshed.

Esau recovered first and slapped his brother on the shoulder and patted his cheek. Jacob wiped the tears from his eyes and kissed the cheek of Esau. Then Esau looked around and surveyed the array of women, children, servants, and livestock scattered across the landscape as his eyes widened in wonder.

"Who are all of these people that come with you?" he asked.

"Let me introduce you," Jacob answered.

He limped to where his family stood uneasily at attention, not knowing whether to trust Esau despite the evidently warm welcome he had just given to his brother.

"Esau, my brother, these are my maids, Bilhah and Zilpah and our children, Leah and our children, and Rachel and our son Joseph."

Esau bowed in greeting and those with Jacob did likewise. The children eyed him warily, not sure of this man that they had been told to flee from, and who now greeted them with apparent friendliness and no ill will.

"And what is this gift that you sent me of flocks and livestock?" Esau asked.

"It is a gift to honor you, brother," Jacob answered.

He bowed again but Esau forestalled him.

"I have plenty of my own, brother. Please, keep what you have."

But Jacob was insistent. He had thought many times over the years of the wrong he had done his brother. His heart had softened when he thought of how he had cheated him over their father's blessing, and now he truly wished to make amends and become friends again.

"Please, Esau; if I have found favor in your sight, then receive what I have given. For your face is as the face of God to me, so earnestly have I wished for a sight of it, and you have received me with favor. God has dealt graciously with me and given me much, far more than I could ever deserve; and I desire to give you a gift from the bounty that God has given me."

Esau searched the face of his brother with a frown creasing his forehead but saw the sincerity of his words. Tears sprang into his eyes, and he looked on the face of Jacob with true affection for the first time since they were boys. Jacob saw it, and a soft smile lit his face as he gazed at his twin with a long dormant affection of his own springing up within his breast. And he realized that he had missed his brother and his companionship...

They nodded at one another and smiled, clapping their hands on each shoulders once more as they did so, and Esau finally relented and gave way to his brother's wishes.

"Very well; I accept your gift. I am honored to do so, brother.

"Now, come and journey with us and I will give you hospitality. For it is a glad day, to be reunited with my brother, and I wish to celebrate."

Jacob was tempted, but for some reason did not feel released to accept his brother's offer, sincere though he believed it to be.

"Thank you, brother, but my children are weary and in need of rest. And my flocks travel slowly. I fear that if we attempt to keep up with you that some of them will die. Please go on ahead of us and we will join you at Seir."

Esau protested at first but could see the sense of Jacob's reasoning and gradually acceded to his plan.

"Then allow me to leave some of my people with you to guide you to Seir, and to be of assistance to you if needed."

But Jacob would not hear of it, and increasingly felt the need to reject the offer that his brother made.

"It is gracious of you, Esau, but I know the way. We shall join you when we are ready."

Esau peered into the face of his brother and in it saw farewell. He was not fooled by the assurance of Jacob and his family joining him at Seir. And in his heart he knew Jacob was right.

Although their reunion was peaceful and had brought consolation to them both, he and his brother could not live together and keep peace. As it had been prophesied before their births, each was to found their own nation, and they would only war for supremacy when they were together.

After Esau's departure Jacob withdrew apart from the others and was thoughtful, remembering the past and feeling a longing to see his father and mother. Would he see them before they departed this world? Only the Lord knew that answer.

He continued on his journey until he came to a broad plain, fertile for grazing. He decided to break their trek here and with the help of his servants erected a house for his family and made booths for his goats, donkeys, and livestock. It would come to be known as Succoth.

It was a peaceful respite and they camped in this place for a season. What a relief it was to at last settle somewhere and end their flight from those who pursued them! The sound of the children's laughter was heard again in the camp, as they played their games and teased their parents, bringing delighted smiles to the faces of their elders. Even the wives were at peace with one another, so glad were they to take a respite from their travels.

But Jacob sensed he was to journey farther into the land of Canaan, and so they eventually packed up their belongings and traveled and came to the city of Shechem. Here he and his family camped before the city gates and lived in peace.

Shechem was a city located where several trade routes crossed, and here Jacob could trade his livestock for grain, olives, and pottery. The citizens were friendly and welcomed strangers in their midst, partly from their temperament and partly because they looked upon all strangers as potential customers for trade.

Jacob knew also that Shechem was part of his family history. For it was here that his grandfather Abram had made a covenant with the Lord. Abram had built an altar to the Lord, and the Lord had promised to give all the land of Canaan to his descendants. Thus it was that Shechem became a hallowed place to the family of Abram.

Jacob mused on the promise made to Abram and to his descendants. He knew that it was here that Abram had believed beyond all reason for believing that he and his aged wife would conceive and bring forth a son that would ever after be regarded as the child of promise. And so because of their faith Jacob's own father Isaac was born and received the mantle of leadership from his father Abram, whom the Lord had sworn to make a father of many nations. That mantle would one day pass to Jacob, who would then pass it to one of his own sons.

As he pondered on the history of his family he felt the need to make some affirmation of his own to carry on that legacy, and to honor the God of his fathers who had blessed him so richly, despite his failures and shortcomings that had brought so much pain to those who bore him, and to his brother who had been supplanted by his ambition. He thought also of the Man with whom he had wrestled, and who had given him a new name, one that did not reflect his old nature, the supplanter, the cheat, but the man that he had become through his trials and suffering and overcoming...

And so it was here that Jacob bought a piece of land where he erected an altar to the God Who was never Named. And he called the altar El-Elohe-Israel, and proclaimed it loud and clear.

"Here is the altar to God, the God of Israel!"

Chapter 16
Vengeance

It was here that tragedy struck.

Dinah was growing up into a tall and strikingly lovely maiden, looking older than her years. She resembled her mother Leah and had inherited Leah's gentle nature and peaceful disposition as well. She quickly made friends with the other maidens of the city and was very popular among them.

If she had only escaped the notice of Shechem all would have been well.

Shechem was the son of Hamor the Hivite, who ruled over the land and the city of Shechem, for which he was named. He was a romantic young man, who lacked common sense and acted on impulse once too often; and that once too often was the day he noticed Dinah the daughter of Jacob. That day would become his downfall.

One day as Dinah was returning from visiting friends, she encountered Shechem, who was immediately smitten by her beauty. She resembled her mother Leah, but was not afflicted with the disfigured eyelids that marred her mother's appearance, and was deemed a lovely young girl. She possessed large soft brown eyes like the eyes of a doe, and rich brown curls that seemed to have a life of their own, springing up when touched and bouncing when her hair was unbound.

Dinah was startled by the appearance of

Shechem in her path, and disconcerted by his obvious admiration. She dropped her head and cast down her eyes in the demure manner deemed appropriate of maidenly modesty, and bowed low to the ground. She waited for Shechem to pass so that she could continue her walk to her father's house, but he was determined to accompany her.

This unexpected encounter flustered Dinah, who was shy around young men, and she stammered in answer to the Prince's reply.

"I am Dinah, the daughter of Jacob and Leah," she answered him. "Please, sir, I beg you to allow me to continue on my way."

But Shechem merely displayed the impetuosity for which he was known, and taking Dinah by the elbow, steered her into a nearby copse of olive trees. The girl paled with alarm; she knew that no proper young girl was ever alone with a man and she quaked and sought a way to escape the unwelcome attentions of this stranger. In addition, she was too young to be presented as an eligible maiden to any young man and was terrified by the persistence of this one.

Shechem saw the alarm in the girl's face and it disturbed him. Maidens always welcomed his attentions, so why was this one different? Her resistance to his charms just made him all the more determined to win her heart and make his conquest.

"Dinah," he whispered as he caught up one of her brown curls and wound it around his finger, "I want us to become better acquainted. We could become very good friends, if you will just cooperate."

He smiled at her to reassure her, but the girl panicked and her fright was clearly evident on her countenance. She stepped back from him and searched frantically for a way to escape. But Shechem was too fast for her.

He caught her by the arms and pulled her to him. Dinah opened her mouth to scream but he clapped a hand over it. She struggled against him but he threw her to the ground, and before she could stop him he had taken her by force after first brutally subduing her.

When it was over she lay sobbing and begged him to go. But Shechem was overcome with tenderness for her and stroked her hair and kissed her lips.

"Don't cry, Dinah," he whispered in her ear, "I shall make it all right. I shall go to your father and ask for your hand. You shall be my wife. Will that not make you happy?

"I shall speak to my father at once."

Dinah did not wait to hear anything further but stumbled to her feet and ran as fast as she could away from the young Prince and back to the home of her parents.

Leah and Jacob were stunned and horrified when Dinah told them of how the young Prince had raped her, acting as if it were his right to do as he pleased to her. Leah caught the sobbing girl to her breast and her tears mingled with her daughter's. Jacob felt a murderous rage overcome him, and the desire to take Shechem by the throat and squeeze the life out of him overpowered him until he forced himself to fight his fury and remain calm that he might plan a course of action.

His sons were still at work in the field. He knew that they would be enraged at this insult to their sister and to their family, and had to determine which course of action to take before they returned and heard of the outrage that had been committed on their sister. He pondered and decided to slip away to pray when he was informed by a servant that Hamor and his son came to call.

Jacob exchanged a surprised glance with Leah, who shrugged her shoulders. The dilemma of how to handle this unexpected visit by their daughter's assailant and his father was plain in both of their faces. Yet they had no choice but to meet their royal visitors.

Hamor bowed to Jacob and Leah and stated the purpose for his visit.

"My son Shechem has just informed me that he loves your daughter Dinah and wishes to take her as his wife immediately. Please make him happy and let it be so."

Shechem nodded his head at Jacob and Leah to confirm the accuracy of the statement and smiled ingratiatingly at them as if this was a normal offer of marriage and that the vile rape had never happened.

Jacob looked into the face of his daughter's rapist and felt disgust and a fierce desire to do violence to the young man surge up within him. He gnashed his teeth together and was about to speak hot words of repudiation when he looked up and saw that his sons had returned from the fields. The face of his eldest revealed all too clearly that they had heard already the news of Dinah's rape.

Hamor now turned a gracious smile upon them.

"Ah, the brothers of my son's intended! How proud you must be of them," he said.

Then he turned back to Jacob and spread wide his hands.

"Come and be part of our people. Give us your daughter to marry my son, and allow your sons to take our daughters in marriage. Then we shall be true neighbors and live in peace together."

He beamed upon Jacob and his sons with the assurance of one who has never had a wish denied, and nodded his head to encourage them to accept his counsel. Jacob sat impassive, not trusting himself to respond in a civilized manner to Hamor's proposition.

It was now Shechem's turn to speak.

"If my offer has found favor in your sight, then I will give whatever you ask as the bridal price," he said to Jacob with a perfunctory nod to Leah. "But give me Dinah to be my bride."

Reuben glanced almost unobtrusively at Simeon, who raised an eyebrow and gave a sidelong glance to Judah, who turned slightly to Dan, who closed his eyes and opened them again at Reuben. This appeared to satisfy Reuben and he acted as spokesman for his brothers when he addressed Hamor.

"I am afraid that we cannot give our consent, for this man is uncircumcised, and that would disgrace our people. There is only one way in which we could give our sister to this man, or intermarry with your people: that is if every man of your city will consent to be circumcised. Then we will give our daughters to you and take your daughters for our brides.

"If you do no agree to this condition, then we will refuse to allow this man to marry our sister."

Although taken aback at the unusual condition that must be met in order for Dinah to be released as a bride, Shechem and Hamor immediately agreed and hastened to call the men of the city. They assembled in the city square and awaited the order of their royal master. When the reason for the assembly was revealed, they could not have been more stunned or alarmed.

"We wish the family of Jacob to continue to dwell in our land and trade with our people, and for his family to marry our daughters. But they will only consent to this on one condition; that every man be circumcised just as they are.

"We urge you to do this, so that we can live in harmony together."

Three days had passed since Hamor and Shechem had urged the men of the city to be circumcised. They had all complied, although unwillingly, and were now in the depths of great pain, and therefore did not attend to their usual business.

Dinah had been taken to the home of Hamor, there to be wed to Shechem when he healed from the circumcision. She was not happy about it, and had wept profusely and begged her father not to make her go, but Jacob had consented rather than to have her remain unmarried due to her shame, which was not her fault, but would count against her nevertheless in the estimation of any who might chance to hear of the rape.

The city gates were opened wide for the usual traffic that came in and out every day. The guards were not alerted when two young men strolled in appearing peaceful and carefree.

Just a couple of lads from the country, here to enjoy a taste of city life, one thought. They look harmless enough, thought the other, may as well let them in and savor our city.

With this reasoning the guards permitted the young men to enter. There was a flash of metal and in the blink of an eye the throats of the guards were cut before they could even cry out.

Through the city cry after cry arose as men recovering from the knife and too weak to defend themselves were run through with the sword. Hamor and Shechem did not escape, royalty though they might be, but paid with their lives for their insult to the house of Jacob, and Dinah was removed from Shechem's house and taken back to her father's.

Nothing and no one escaped the looting as the two young men purged the city. With the men all dead there was no one to defend the women and children and livestock, and all were herded together and marched away behind their captors.

Jacob's outrage knew no bounds when news of the atrocity came to his ears. At first he could not believe the report that was given to him. But his own servants testified to witnessing two of his sons bring back a great group of women and children, with livestock following behind.

One of his servants ventured to approach him.

"I bring news, grave news, master," the old man said softly with a quaver in his voice.

For some reason Jacob felt a qualm before the news was even related. He had not liked the way his sons had looked at each other when they had received their royal visitors...

"Yes?" Jacob inquired, as he lifted one eyebrow at the servant.

"Reuben!" he shouted for his eldest.

Jacob rampaged through the camp, bellowing until his oldest son answered his call and appeared before him.

"What have you done!" Jacob roared.

Reuben did not need to be told, having already heard the news himself.

"I did nothing, Father," he said. "But don't think that the thought did not cross my mind. But I feared putting Dinah at risk should news of the attack be discovered and the alarm sounded and she slain in retaliation before we reached the king's house."

"Then who..."

Jacob confronted his sons Simeon and Levi.

"What have you done? You have made my name odious to all the inhabitants of Canaan by your foul deed! Indeed, you have smeared it with dishonor! I came in peace to live among them, and you have destroyed the men and enslaved the women and children, treating them like cattle with no value.

"Now the Canaanites and Perizzites will strike me and my house and we shall be destroyed! All of us wiped out from the face of the earth!

"What madness possessed you?"

He shook with fury as his face reddened to the color of a poppy in the fields. But the young men stood their ground and did not flinch as they stared into their father's face.

It was Simeon who ultimately took responsibility for their actions.

"Trouble we may have stirred, and trouble we may yet see," he said in a firm voice that did not break or quiver in the face of his father's rage.

"But we cannot allow anyone, even a Prince, to treat our sister like a harlot."

Chapter 17
A New Name

Jacob knew that any hope of living peacefully in Shechem among his neighbors was now destroyed after the massacre his sons had so cruelly and unfairly inflicted on the inhabitants. Such a monstrous attack unprovoked by an innocent people filled him with shame. He rued their impetuosity and knew they had inherited it from him, as their mother Leah was always calm and gentle. She grieved with him, and their dismay over their sons' misdeeds and the rape of their daughter drew them closer together.

He had come to appreciate her quiet ways and sweet voice that knew how to soothe not only the children with tender lullabies, but himself with softly whispered words of encouragement that calmed him when he felt turmoil within. Even in the days of his betrothal to Rachel when he had labored for her father he had sought Leah out occasionally because of her serene nature that soothed him and her common sense that helped him to see things in perspective.

Now it was he who comforted her, knowing how the slaughter of their neighbors grieved not only them but the Lord, and wondered what punishment their sons might reap for their murderous deeds.

"How could we have known what our sons would do, Leah?" he soothed her. "Who could have foreseen such a thing? They themselves suggested the circumcision, and even I thought that they told the truth; that they would accept the offer for Dinah to save her reputation, and intermarriage with the daughters of the city in return for meeting the condition. In truth, I was alarmed that they would even consider intermarriage, but this is far worse, to strike the innocent without warning when they were unable to defend themselves."

His statement was greeted by a fresh storm of weeping from Leah, who could not shake the picture of strong but helpless men struck down before they could raise arms to save their lives, and of their innocent wives and defenseless children marched off to captivity. Simeon and Levi had refused to return their spoils, and had taken the women and children to a nearby settlement where they sold them as slaves, and sold all of the livestock as well, and so had greatly enriched themselves with the plunder they had taken.

But Jacob was heartsick, and knew he could remain no longer to be a reproach in the eyes of his neighbors in the land around them.

"Go to Bethel," the Lord said to him in a vision when he inquired for guidance and counsel. "And erect an altar to Me, Who appeared to you there when you fled from your brother, Esau."

Jacob therefore assembled his household; his wives, children, and servants to reveal the plan that the Lord had given him.

"You must consecrate yourself," he

commanded them. "Remove any idols from among you; do not bow down to them, for they are not God. There is but one God, the Lord is His Name.

"Purify your hearts and rid yourself of those sins that would hinder you in obeying God. Change your garments and put on clean robes and sandals for your feet.

"For we are traveling to Bethel and I will erect there an altar to the God Who saved me in my distress and has never left me through all the days of my life. He has been with me wherever I went, and carried me in all that befell me. He has never forgotten me, and this altar will be a memorial to Him, for as long as men live on the earth."

The servants did as he bade them to and brought to him all of their idols, and any jewelry in their possession that had been dedicated in idolatry; charms of images of gods that dangled from bracelets, rings with the inscription of an idol's name, and rings worn through the nose to symbolize dedication to a particular god. Nothing was held back, but all hastened to obey. When he had collected all that was brought to him Jacob buried all of it under an old oak tree near the city limits of Shechem.

Before they left Rachel sought him out and spoke earnestly with him.

"Jacob," she began, "I have searched my heart for any wrong that I feel, and I am sure that the rest of our household has done the same. Just look at how zealously the servants have brought everything dedicated to idols and renounced them!"

Jacob smiled at her.

"Indeed, they have," he agreed.

She nodded her head somewhat absently.

"I do wonder sometimes, though," she said casually, and waited for his response.

Jacob glanced at her with a frown between his eyes as he lifted one eyebrow in inquiry.

"What do you wonder?" he asked.

"Oh, nothing," she said hastily.

Then she seemed to change her mind and spoke again.

"Do you ever wonder?" she asked, and then stopped abruptly.

"Wonder about what?" Jacob asked with growing curiosity.

It was not like Rachel to be hesitant; far too often she spoke first and later considered the impact of her words. It was not unusual for her words to offend those around her when she spoke in haste, so this hesitancy stoked his curiosity greatly.

Rachel began again, and then stopped and wrung her hands, much to her husband's amusement.

What on earth ailed his wife!

Rachel took a deep breath, and then seemed to resolve some conflict within herself. She turned to look at Jacob before answering his question.

"Well," she stammered, "speaking of idols, do you ever wonder who stole my father's teraphim when we fled from him?"

"Oh," Jacob answered.

He meditated on the question and realized that he had nearly forgotten the incident. Nothing further had ever come of it and no idols had ever materialized, and so it had slipped his mind completely.

"No, I can't say that I ever gave it a second thought, except to think that your father must have been mistaken and the thief was a servant in his own household."

"Well, you would think so," Rachel said, as her color heightened and her words tumbled together, "as our servants and all of us have enjoyed excellent health; and you said that whoever had taken the idols would die. That sounded rather like a curse, you know."

"I suppose it was," Jacob responded. "It is bad enough to consult idols, but to steal them from someone who worships them seems even worse. It is like robbing of a man of that which he considers holy, whether it actually is or not. To treat a man's belief in such a fashion is to proclaim that you do not revere any deity yourself. It is one thing to declare a deity a false idol and destroy it for the pretender it is, but another to steal away what another worships and do with it what you will."

Rachel flushed at this statement and chose to ignore its implications, but instead remained fixed on her purpose for bringing up the incident.

"Do you believe in curses, Jacob?" Rachel asked abruptly.

She shot a glance at him from beneath lowered lids and studied him covertly for his reaction.

"Yes, I do," he nodded his head without hesitation.

"Do you believe that they come to pass?" she asked as her voice rose slightly.

"Oh, yes, I do!" he answered. "For words spoken can not be revoked, whether they are curses or blessings. There is great power in what we say, Rachel, both for good and for harm, and much of our destiny is shaped by the words that escape our lips, if only we knew it."

Rachel blinked her eyes and turned pale but Jacob had his head averted from her and did not see it.

When all had searched their hearts and their belongings for anything that might grieve the Lord they came to Jacob and presented themselves before him. He was pleased with the obedience of his servants and family and felt they were at last ready. So he summoned his household together and bade them pack up their belongings, for they would not be returning to this place again; and so they began their journey.

Wherever they traveled men whispered in fear.

"There they go; Jacob and his family. It is said that they are under the protection of a powerful God, One more powerful than any other known to man. If any dare to harm them, this God will see it and repay the evil that was done. Therefore we must let them journey unmolested, or it will be us who pays the forfeit."

And so Jacob and his family were left in

peace as they journeyed from Shechem to Bethel.

Jacob looked at the land in front of him. How well he remembered, as if it were only yesterday! And yet it had been so long ago...

He recalled the day he had fled from the wrath of his brother Esau, running for his life.

"I will kill you!" Esau thundered, when he learned of the stolen blessing bestowed by their father upon Jacob, following on the heels of forcing him to sell his birthright when he was hungry and desperate for food to restore his strength.

"Go Jacob," his mother Rebekah had urged him, "take flight before your brother makes good his promise and murders you!"

He had run and run and run, and been set upon by thieves who stole everything in his possession, including the bridal dowry his mother had given him when he left, even in her anxiety conscious of the price he must pay for a bride. The robbers had taken everything he owned but for the clothes on his back; and so for seven years he had been forced to work for Laban to take Rachel as his bride, and then another seven to serve for both her and Leah when she had been forced upon him through trickery by her father.

He had come to this place, exhausted, heartbroken, and half dead from lack of food and water. Indeed, he had wished to die, and had sunk to the ground with a desire to never rise back up. He remembered with bitterness all of the actions he had taken that had brought him to his place, and rued every one of them, so much that he decided life was not worth living and he wished to be done with it.

But God had met him in this place. In a vision of the night He spoke to him and revealed a ladder that had run from Heaven to the earth, and spoken to him, and promised to make him a great nation if he would obey and serve the God of Abraham and Isaac.

Jacob stood in silence, remembering, his ears pricked up as if listening intently for something that no one else could hear. And then he picked up the first stone.

He built a mighty pillar, one stone placed atop the other until it reached for the sky. When he had erected the altar he stood in front of it, his head bowed low and his arms lifted high, and waited for the presence of the Lord to come to him. He felt a gentle breeze stirring around him even as a warmth seemed to descend upon him and knew that his vigil was not in vain.

"Jacob," the Lord called, "for so your name has been called; Jacob, the cheat, the supplanter, and so you have been. But you will be called Jacob no longer. Your name is Israel, for you have contended with God.

"I am God Almighty.

"Be fruitful and multiply, for a nation and a company of nations shall come from you, and kings shall come from your children. All the land that I promised to Abraham and Isaac I will give to you and to those who come after you."

And then the Lord left him and all was quiet.

In the place where God had spoken to him and made a promise for his descendants Jacob set up a pillar as a monument. He poured a drink offering on it and then poured oil over it.

"This place shall be called Bethel," he intoned solemnly, "for it is the house of God."

Chapter 18
The Lastborn

They had journeyed but a little way and had not yet reached Bethlehem when Rachel cried out in pain. Those nearest her tugged on the reins of their camels and stopped in their tracks and turned to her in alarm, knowing that her child was due at any time.

"Jacob!" she screamed.

He whipped his head around and moved his camel close to hers, taking her by the hand and gazing anxiously into her eyes. They were wide and her face pale; beads of sweat had formed upon her forehead, and she trembled upon her camel.

"My time has come," Rachel announced.

And then she slid from the back of the beast before Jacob could catch her and collapsed to the ground.

It was a long and difficult labor, and the entire camp was fraught with tension. Not being able to journey further they had set up the tents and made Rachel as comfortable as was possible under the less than ideal circumstances. All day she cried out and screamed in agony but the baby seemed perversely determined to come in his own time and not accede to the calendar that proclaimed the time of his birth was due.

Fear assailed Rachel and would not loose its grip.

"I shall die, and the babe with me," she

confided to the midwife who had accompanied them, knowing that Rachel's time was near and that she might well have the baby on the journey.

"No, no, that is not true," the midwife replied in an effort to calm the terrified young woman.

"Yes, I shall die," Rachel insisted, "and the babe shall die with me."

"No, you are mistaken," the midwife said again. "It is merely a difficult birth; that is all. You and the babe shall both pull through, and how happy you will be when it comes into the world!"

Yet the midwife was concerned, and had good cause to be. Rachel was now thirty-six, past the flush of youth and the prime child bearing years when she should be in her best physical condition. And she had been barren for so long and had carried only one child until now, a factor that concerned the midwife greatly.

But the midwife soothed Rachel and bathed her clammy brow in cool cloths with water brought from a nearby spring and attempted to have her focus on the impending birth and the joy it would bring.

"It is true that it will be a happy day," Rachel agreed. "How I have longed for children, with none but my little Joseph to call my own. Jacob will be so proud, especially if this child is another boy. I pray it is, for when I delivered Joseph I asked God to give me one more."

"There, you see," the midwife responded, "and He has heard your prayers and answered them."

The child had come, strong and healthy, kicking with all of the energy of his older brothers and giving a lusty cry when slapped on his bottom. Jacob exulted in this, his twelfth son, no less than he had his first, and the child's brothers came into the chamber after the birth to marvel at his arrival.

But Rachel cried out and moaned even after the child was born.

"Jacob," she whispered. "Jacob, come here."

The sight of her pale face alarmed him; she seemed strangely drained of all color, and her strength appeared to have deserted her.

He hastened to her side, and bid the others to leave them. The boys exited without any word of protest and still smiled at the arrival of another brother. Leah bit her bottom lip, but shed a glance of concern upon her vital sister who lay so pale and listless in her bed.

When they were alone Jacob took Rachel's hand and kissed it. He stroked it softly and smoothed back the wet strands of black hair that clung to her clammy forehead. Rachel moaned softly and seemed to take comfort in his ministrations, then began to weep quietly.

"What is it, my love?" he whispered as he took her hand and kissed it once again.

"Oh, Jacob, I am leaving you," she whispered.

"No; no!" he exclaimed in a voice roughened by a sudden fear at the pallor of her face and the strange listlessness that she exhibited.

"Yes, I am going to die, Jacob. Something was wrong with this birth; I felt something was amiss even when we were on the road. I have an injury of some sort, and I shall not recover."

Jacob knew it was possible and had counted himself fortunate that Leah had made it safely through the deliveries of all seven of her children. But Rachel could not die; not after all they had been through together! And especially when she had just given him another son, as they had hoped and yearned for so long...

"Jacob," she whispered again. "Know that I love you. Nothing ever destroyed that love, not the years of waiting, or sharing you with my sister, or the barrenness. It was always you I loved, and no other."

A sob erupted from his throat and tears unexpectedly gushed down his cheeks but he did not wipe them away. She could not leave him!

"Take our son, Jacob," she said, and handed him the child. "His name is Ben-oni, for he is the son of my sorrow. Tell him about me in the years to come, and how much I loved him and longed for his coming. Tell him that, Jacob."

Jacob began to weep softly.

"I will tell him that, my love," he promised. "But his name shall be Benjamin, for he will be the son of my right hand."

For a moment the tent was filled with the sound of their weeping as they became resigned to their long parting. Although Jacob loathed to admit it, he saw death in his beloved's face, a death that he could not save her from.

"I have something to confess, Jacob,"

Rachel said with her last bit of strength. "It was I who stole Father's teraphim. I did not want him tracking us, and so I stole them. And now I am going to die, just as you said the one who had stolen them would do."

Jacob gasped and turned as white as the tops of the mountains in winter when they are laden with snow.

"No!" he cried out. "How can that be?"

"You cursed me," she answered. "You did not mean to, but you did."

He shook his head slowly, remembering the incident and never dreaming that he cursed the one dearer to him than any other. Then he shook his head again and hastened to comfort Rachel.

"But that was some time ago," he assured her, "and you are just now dying. You cannot be dying due to a curse!"

"Oh, but I am," she said. "Remember what you said once about blessings and curses and how they can not be revoked?

"However, my death did not happen at once because I received great mercy. I had prayed after the birth of Joseph for God to give me another son, and He has. So He delayed my death until I had give birth today, so that my prayer and petition to Him was granted.

"But now I am going to die, Jacob, just as I knew I would. And I bid you farewell, my love. Take care of our boys."

And with these words, Rachel breathed her last.

Chapter 19
Family Matters

With the unexpected passing of his beloved brought about by his own careless words Jacob felt old suddenly and picked up his tents, gathered what remained of his family and moved on.

He had erected a stately monument to Rachel on the road to Bethlehem. It rose as a stone pillar and soared to the sky. Forever it would mark the place of her burial, and where his heart was broken. But he knew that he would never be able to look on the site again.

Leah thought with sadness of her sister, and wished that things had turned out differently. How close they had been and how deep the affection between them before their father had tricked Joseph into marrying her; and how bitterly they had vied for the love of their husband! And how many children had come into the world because of their rivalry for Jacob's heart!

And yet, they were sisters, and Leah had yearned for the companionship that only a sister could give. No other woman except one's mother was the recipient of intimate confidences, and no other woman could fully understand another except the one with whom she had shared a household and a family and experienced the same upbringing. Only Rachel could understand the pain that the deception of their father had brought to Leah's heart in forcing her to marry

Jacob. But the very act had severed the bond of sisterhood between them, never to be restored.

And now her sister was gone.

They had reached Edar, where a tower of stones was erected that dominated the landscape and decided to make camp for a while. Jacob frequently separated himself from the rest, taking long walks and praying to the Lord for comfort in his grief. He did not visit Leah in the night, and she knew he was mourning the loss of Rachel. She made no complaint or inquiry but waited patiently for his grief to subside and for him to seek her company once again.

Leah could not have known that more than grief tormented Jacob. He thought of the blessing from his father that he had stolen from his brother Esau, and that it was this very act that had driven him from his father's house in fear for his life. If it were true that the deeds of a man's hands returned to him, was it possible that his inadvertent cursing of his beloved wife and her subsequent death was in return a punishment that stole from him his dearest possession?

Such thoughts made Jacob's days dark indeed.

The news that was brought to Jacob made his blood boil.

Reuben had taken his father's concubine Bilhah and slept with her as casually as if she had been a prostitute he had hired for the night.

160

How could he insult his father in such a fashion! What ailed these older sons of his; Simeon and Levi murdering their neighbors and Reuben insulting his father's manhood by confiscating one of his concubines for his own use!

Jacob did not trust himself to discipline his son, fearful that he might retaliate with violence. He kept quiet about the matter, and pretended to have no knowledge of it, but the day of reckoning for Reuben would come. Of that he would make certain.

At last the day came when Jacob came to Mamre where he was reunited with his father Isaac. Although it was no more than a large grove of trees, Jacob looked on the site with awe, for it was here that his grandfather Abram was said to have received the angels that brought him news of his own father Isaac's imminent conception and pregnancy by his wife Sarai. It was as a holy place he regarded it, and he treated it as such. He took off his sandals and bade those that were with him to do the same.

It was with great trepidation that he approached his father. The old man was now one hundred and eighty years old, a great age that few ever reached. Jacob found himself remembering the unusual circumstances of his father's birth and the strange events that had happened later, which had been related to him by Isaac.

"My father was an old man with no heir for his line, and although he and his wife Sarai had tried desperately for children, it was all in vain,"

Isaac had told him. "But one day the Lord appeared to Abram, as he was then called, and spoke to him, and promised to make him a father of many nations.

"As the sands of the seashore, as many as the stars in the sky, so shall your descendants be, too numerous to count," the Lord told him.

"But Sarai was barren, and it was hard to believe that she could bear a child at her age. Indeed, she laughed when Abram told her the news, and the Lord said that the baby would be called Isaac, which means laughter. And it was due to Sarai's unbelief that everything became muddled.

"She did not believe it was possible for her to bear a child, so she suggested to my father Abram that he take her Egyptian maid Hagar as a wife to his bed, and the child conceived and born on her knees as she assisted in the birth would be counted as hers. He was reluctant, because he truly believed the word of the Lord, that He would perform what He had promised, but he obeyed to please his wife.

"It was inevitable, I suppose, that when Hagar conceived she despised her mistress and mocked her to her face. Sarai was enraged and drove the girl out of the house with her cruelty. Hagar wept in the wilderness where the Lord found her and told her to go back and serve her mistress faithfully, and He would bless her child.

"Back she went, and in time her son Ishmael was born. But Sarai resented it, and now earnestly believed the word of the Lord that she would have a child, but it would be several years before it came to pass.

"When it did, Hagar and Ishmael ridiculed me, and were cruel, to such an extent that my mother Sarai, whose name was now Sarah, asked my father, whose name had been changed to Abraham, to get rid of her and her son once and for all.

"And so they were cast out and I never saw my brother again except for when we buried our father together when he departed the world."

Jacob reflected on his father's words. Strange this strife between brothers sounded similar to that of his with his brother, Esau. Was there a strain that ran in particular families, or was it peculiar to his alone? Even his wives had been placed in the position of rivals for their husband's favor, just as he and his brother had vied for the favor of their mother and father, and Isaac and Ishmael had fought for the preeminence of their father's household. Was it possible that one action begat another action, and that just as seeds brought forth from their own kind, that actions spawned traits that were passed down through the generations?

He found the thought disturbing, and so kept it to himself.

He looked at the blind old man in front of him and a lone tear traveled down his face unchecked to the neckline of his robe. Leah stood beside him and stole a soft hand around his arm, comforting him. He reached over and patted her hand in silent gratitude, and then locked her fingers with his.

"And now both of my sons are here, and I have my heart's wish granted," Isaac stated as he huffed in satisfaction. "And you have large families, both of you!"

"Yes, Father," Esau replied with a face that reflected his deep and tender love for the old man. "Jacob and I each have been blessed with twelve sons, and daughters as well."

"Ah, that will make of each of you a mighty nation," Isaac responded with a sparkle of joy in his faded eyes. "For that was prophesied over both of you when you were yet in your mother's womb."

Rebekah's smile was a soft glow that lit the room as she beheld her two sons on either side of their father, a sight she had never thought to see again.

"Yes, I remember," she said. "And how you boys have grown to have such large families of your own. Why, you each have a tribe apiece!"

Laughter erupted in the room, a rare sound in their family, and one they were not altogether comfortable with. Leah sensed that this room had known angry words and sorrowful tears, but laughter was a stranger with which it was not familiar. She silently prayed to the Lord for healing to strengthen the bonds of brotherhood.

"The Lord is good," Isaac began to intone.

His sons snapped to attention.

"There is but One God, and the Lord is His Name. Gracious and merciful is He, and His love endures forever," they joined with the old man.

The tomb was freshly cut in the nearby cave and all was ready. Isaac had been anointed with fragrant spices and wrapped in fine linen, and was to be laid to rest next to his father Abraham and his mother Sarah. His sons Jacob and Esau came with their mother Rebekah to lay his mortal remains to rest.

As the brothers stood together at the tomb weeping there were no words adequate to comfort their sorrow. Each knew they had let their father down; Esau with his marriages to Canaanite women, and Jacob with his treatment of his brother and flight from home with the long absence that followed.

Now they stood together silently, staring at the rock that had been rolled into place to seal the tomb.

Esau inhaled slowly and let out a deep sigh as he wiped the tears from the corner of his eyes.

"I shall miss him," he stated. "In spite of everything, I loved him and he loved me."

"Yes," Jacob answered. "That is true; and I have no doubt that Father took much comfort in the memory of that love over the years when we were gone. It is I who grieved him the most, and I only hope that I have made some atonement by seeing him before he was laid to rest with his fathers.

"But I may never know."

Chapter 20
The Blessing

The old man lay in his bed dying. His family was hastening to gather around him and bid him farewell, but while he waited he remembered...

Remembered the years when his beloved Joseph had been presumed dead, torn by wild animals, and the agony his heart had endured at the thought of his perishing through so violent a death. Joseph had been his favorite of all of his twelve sons, the firstborn of Rachel, and as a mark of his favor he had presented him with a multi-colored robe that Joseph wore proudly and flaunted unthinkingly before his brothers.

He would never forget the day when his sons had come to him and told him that Joseph's blood-stained robe had been found, torn from his body. They assumed he had been devoured by a wild beast, for no other trace of him had ever been found.

He felt as he had in the days when Rachel died, that a light had gone out and life would never be worth living again. How dark and empty his days had been at that time, and how long the recovery until he could enjoy life again and take his part in the world around him. But he had found solace in this son of hers, and now he was taken from him as well.

How great had been his joy when his sons had journeyed to the land of Egypt during the great famine to buy grain and had found to their great astonishment their younger brother now ruling the land, second in command only to Pharaoh himself. How proud Jacob had been, and how overjoyed to have his son restored to him from the dead. In haste he had traveled to see his son, so eager that he did not feel the discomfort of the journey, and how sweet was their reunion.

Yes, it was incredible that this son had been raised to such a position of power and prominence. But Jacob had been heartbroken to discover that his sons had lied to him about their brother's death.

What bitter rivalry ran in his family, he reflected. His father Isaac with his half brother Ishmael, his own battle for supremacy with his brother Esau, even the jealous contending for his love by his two wives, and culminating in the murderous hatred that his sons felt for their own brother because of Jacob's favoritism. Was Joseph's years of suffering at the hands of his brothers his fault for favoring him so blatantly that his brothers could no longer endure it, or due to some character weakness that had been passed down from one generation to the next?

They had been contrite, and Joseph himself had assured all of them that wrong though their actions had been, the hand of the Lord had led him here, so that he would be in a position to save their family from starvation during the time of the great famine that ravaged their land.

They had settled in Egypt, but Jacob knew that this was not where they belonged. But while the famine held sway in Canaan it seemed wise to remain near a bountiful food supply, and so the children of Israel stayed...

"Father," Joseph whispered, the tears brimming in his eyes, "I am here. I came at your summons, and am willing to do whatever you desire."

"Joseph," Jacob whispered back, "I am content now that I have seen you. I want you to make me a promise."

"What is it, Father?" Joseph asked, his voice eager and ready to please the old man he loved so much.

"I am dying," Jacob answered. "And I want you to promise not to bury me here in Egypt where I do not belong; but carry my body out of Egypt and bury me with my fathers."

"I promise, Father," Joseph answered. "I swear it shall be done."

They were all assembled now, the twelve sons of Jacob, born of his wives, Leah and Rachel, and his concubines Bilhah and Zilpah. They waited to be admitted to their father's presence with mixed emotions, not knowing what to expect; for the old man was unpredictable and each had a unique relationship with this unusual man. They whispered among themselves as to what they thought the outcome might be.

"It will all go to Joseph; we know that," sighed Reuben.

Firstborn though he was he was all too painfully aware that Joseph was still their father's favorite, his pride in this son only increased through his elevation in Egypt after being sold into slavery by his brothers, a deed which did not raise any of them in the estimation of their father.

One by one they agreed with Reuben. Joseph was the old man's favorite, and everything would go to him. There was no point in wondering who would inherit their father's mantle for it was a foregone conclusion.

Jacob did not keep them in suspense for very long.

He began by remembering back to all that had happened in his life, how he had been driven from his father's house by the wrath of his brother Esau, only to wander to the house of Laban, where he met and married his wives, who bore his sons to him. Then they had left the house of Laban and encountered his brother Esau, with whom he had been reconciled. On the way to Canaan his beloved Rachel had died and been buried on the road to Bethlehem. And in Canaan he had been reunited with his father and together with his brother Esau laid him to rest with their people.

"And through it all the God of Abraham and Isaac was faithful to me," Jacob told them. "He brought me through many trials, and gave me many blessings, and it was His hand that led me all through my long life. I praise Him and no other."

Here they bowed their heads and gave silent adoration to the Lord.

"And now," Jacob said, "before my

strength fails me I wish to address my sons."

It was the moment they had waited for; some dreaded it, some were assured that they had done nothing but good to their father and had nothing to fear by way of rebuke.

"Reuben, my eldest, my firstborn," Jacob began, "you were my first son to see the light of day, and as the firstborn you should have the preeminence over your brothers, as is usual and customary. But I regret to say that you are as unstable as boiling water. You defiled my bed by taking my concubine for yourself, and it shall cost you your inheritance."

Reuben gasped at the disclosure of knowledge that he thought had been concealed from his father but Jacob did not wait for him to speak. He held up a hand to silence his son and went on.

"Simeon and Levi, you are next in line; you are brothers of violence, deceitful and cruel, and with your swords you spilled the blood of our neighbors who were at peace with us. You dishonored me with your plot and brought shame upon my good name. Your anger is cursed for its ill foundation and your wrath against the innocent was cruel. I will divide you and scatter you abroad so that you may not join forces to do evil again."

The two brothers looked at each other in dismay. They knew they had infuriated their father with the incident at Shechem, indeed, he never let them forget it; but how could he divide them after he was dead?

"Judah, you are worthy of praise and your hand shall be on the necks of your enemies as you lay them in the dust," Jacob intoned. "All of your family will bow down to you, and honor your name and the scepter will not depart from Judah until the coming of Shiloh, the mighty King. You are my heir to the mantle of leadership for our tribe, and all that I possess is yours."

A gasp ran through the assembly. Judah's face lit with surprised delight at his father's words. The rest glanced at Joseph, who did not appear surprised at the announcement, but stood with bowed head as tears of grief trickled silently down his handsome face.

Jacob continued to allot their portions to his sons as if the interruption had not occurred.

"Zebulun shall settle on the coast and be a haven for the ships that come and go to trade. And there you shall prosper and become rich," he declared as Zebulon received the blessing with great joy.

"Issachar is a strong man of labor, and works to make the land his own. Your descendants shall possess their land and know the times and seasons and be consulted for their wisdom."

Issachar nodded his head and crossed his arms over his chest. An honorable legacy, and a valuable one as well. It meant that his family would be held in honor and not have to serve others. Yes, a good legacy, indeed.

"Dan shall judge his people with righteousness and lie in wait for his enemies that he may conquer them," was the pronouncement given to Dan, who greatly appreciated the honor that was bestowed upon him.

"Gad shall be attacked but turn the tables on his enemies and prevail in their midst."

Gad appeared a little disturbed at this statement, but after a moment realized that his father was declaring what he saw and not what he wished for him. Gad would be assailed but would conquer his enemies nevertheless. He smiled in appreciation at his father and bowed his head.

"Asher shall prosper and never know want, the food of his table fit for a king; for the Lord shall grant him the desires of his heart," Jacob stated to the tall son who smiled his gracious thanks to his father with a shimmer of tears in his eyes.

As the son of his father and a concubine he did not feel he had quite the same standing as the brothers who were the offspring of his father's wives, so the blessing was doubly appreciated by him.

"Naphtali is as sure-footed as a deer in the mountains, full of tact and discernment and able to triumph in all trials, and sires lovely daughters."

This statement was met with unexpected laughter by Naphtali's brothers, who were suddenly amused by the brother who invariably put his foot in his mouth rather than told others what they wanted to hear. Clearly their father was declaring what he wished for this son, and not what he saw.

"Joseph is a fruitful bough that feeds many and the blessings of the Almighty rest on him."

At the mention of feeding many, even Joseph's brothers nodded their heads and shot him smiles of appreciation and gratitude. Had it not been for his wisdom and prudence they would all have perished in the great famine that had prevailed in the known world and none of them would be here this day. And suddenly remembering the dream he had shared with them so long ago, they turned as one to him and bowed low.

Jacob turned with tender affection to his youngest son, the one who had cost his beloved Rachel her life when she brought him into the world. How like her in nature he was, vital and energetic, with a ferocious temper that took little to provoke! But what a warrior he was as well, always willing to take up arms, and always looking out for the welfare of others.

"Benjamin is a ravenous wolf who devours his prey in the morning and at night distributes what remains to his people so that they are provided for."

There was a long silence as the old man paused for breath. His strength was now failing rapidly, and tears came to the eyes of those he had blessed, and tears to the eyes of those he had rebuked, as they reflected on the tumultuous years they had lived through with him.

There was the sound of open weeping as those around him suddenly sensed that an era was passing, as the scepter of leadership was being passed to their brother Judah, and the time of Jacob was drawing to its close.

"Gather me to my people, bury me with my fathers in the cave in the field of Ephron the Hittite at Machpelah, east of Mamre in the land of Canaan. It is there where my father buried Abraham and Sarah; it is there where my brother Esau and I buried our father Isaac and our mother Rebekah; and it is there where I buried Leah."

When he had finished his instructions to his many sons, Jacob breathed out silently and his soul went to God.

And in the tomb where he was buried, he lay next to Leah, his wife, the mother of kings from whose descendants would come the great King; and she would lie beside him until the end of time.

L. M. Roth is the pen name of a Christian author from the American Midwest. L. M. Roth is a "pilgrim on the path of life" and a seeker of truth. This quest first began at the age of eight when the author read Little Women and was struck by the sense of destiny shared by each of the March sisters as they "pilgrimed" their way through the trials and thrills that only life can offer. The quest deepened through the exposure to classic mythology and legends, which birthed a sense of hidden identity, that we are not who we have always thought we were, but are each of us heroes and heroines destined for something great and noble.

Who are we? Where are we going? What tasks are we meant to accomplish during our time on Earth? We are all on a journey together as we seek the answers. You may join L. M. Roth in that quest anytime you read one of the author's books.

Books by L. M. Roth include:

Quest For the Kingdom Part I The Legend of the Great Pearl

Quest For the Kingdom Part II Conquering the Domain of Darkness

Quest For the Kingdom Part III Invitation To Eternity

Quest For the Kingdom Part IV A Stranger Among Us

Quest For the Kingdom Part V Rise of the Time of Evil

Quest For the Kingdom Part VI The Sorceress and the Seer

Quest For the Kingdom Part VII A New Kingdom Rises

A Knight's Guide To Spiritual Warfare

A Star In the Darkness Esther and the King of Persia

Abelard and the Dragon's Vapor

Abelard and the Witch's Vengeance

Abelard and the Knights' Vow

Arise My Love The Princess Who Fell Asleep

Battleground: Elijah and the War With Jezebel

Beware My Lady The Princess Who Would Not Wed

Cinderella's Shoe A Fairy Tale Murder Mystery

Come Back My Lord The Princess Who Loved Too Much

Disenchanted In the Land of Dreams Come True

Dragon Slayers and Other Tales From the Perilous Forest

Lights in the Mist and Other Original Fairy Tales and Fairy Tale Spoofs

Christmas Cheer and Other Holiday Stories

Made in the USA
Coppell, TX
07 January 2022

71156098R00098